By the same author

Novels
Méirscrí na Treibhe
Stiall Fhial Feola
An Fear Dána
Amach

Short Stories
Eiriceachtaí agus Scéalta Eile
Fabhalscéalta
Leabhar Nóra Ní Anluain

Plays
Tagann Godot

Critical Works
Máirtín Ó Cadhain: clár saothair
An tÚrscéal Gaeilge
An Cogadh in Aghaidh na Critice
Chun Doirne: rogha aistí
A Pocket History of Gaelic Culture
'Beir leat do shár-Ghaeilge!': súil siar agus ar aghaidh

PARABOLAS

PARABOLAS

Stories & Fables

ALAN TITLEY

LAGAN PRESS
BELFAST
2005

Published by
Lagan Press
editorial.laganpress@verbalartscentre.co.uk
www.laganpress.co

All correspondence to
Lagan Press
Verbal Arts Centre
Stable Lane & Mall Wall
Bishop Street Within
Derry-Londonderry
BT48 6PU

ISBN: 978 1 904652 23 6
Authors: Titley, Alan
Title: Parabolas
Stories & Fables
first published 2005
reprinted with minor corrections 2013

This one is for Fergal

CONTENTS

Introduction

The stories in this book are culled from three previous collections. They were all originally written in Irish so these may be seen as translations, or more correctly, versions of those tales. I prefer to call them versions as I believe that true translation is an impossible dream. Writing in any language takes on the ghosts and hobgoblins of that language and these presences haunt every word and phrase. And pookas and sprites do not easily cross over from one world to another. So these stories do not bear any true equivalences to their Irish origins. They are neither clones nor doublegangers, more likely related changelings playing in their kindredgarden.

But mostly they are stories. While some of them follow the well-rutted path of the traditional short story, there are others that are tales, or yarns, or fables, or plots, or just fictions, because a story is a truly raggy thing. Many of them are mercifully short and others have a touch of the shaggy dog. A story can be as beautifully crafted as a Henry Moore sculpture, or as messy and stodgy as the ooze from the magic porridge pot. This is because the origin of story is of a low-life form. While the poet sits above in the palace and communes with the king or with God, the story-teller wanders in the market place with the snakecharmers and the opium sellers and the pick-pockets and the three-card-trick merchants. No storyteller need ever be ashamed of this bad company-keeping. Some of these shorter pieces were written out of sheer jealousy of the lyric poet who receives wild applause after a few brief lines at a reading while the storyteller has to go on and on and on and on before a polite clap of appreciation might be offered.

Alan Titley
1 February 2005

The Storyteller

ONCE UPON A TIME AND A very long time ago there was a storyteller who came from out of the east telling stories. He would stop people in the street, grab them by the sleeve and whisper coarsely in their ear, 'Hey, did you hear the one about ... ?'

They didn't take much notice of him at first because they thought him odd, and peculiar, and even a little queer. He also had a rough country accent as if he hadn't quite taken the potato out of his mouth. In truth, he was a bit of a hayseed. How could anyone who told stories on street corners or in the fields or in the back rooms of pubs be taken seriously?

But gradually he became a bit of a cult figure. Among a minority of likeminded bumpkins at first, people who enjoyed tales about country life, and sowing seeds, and harvesting apples and going to school through the fields. But when he then started on the stories about whores and prostitutes more of the spivs and the slickers pricked up their ears. He had some pretty good yarns about youths getting pissed and indulging in great bouts of debauchery in the big city as soon as they escaped from the farm.

He also said some weird things that didn't make much

sense but people remembered them because they were catchy and way out. 'If you ever throw a party,' he said once at the end of a story, as these bits were often attached to the main telling, 'if you ever throw a party like the fat capitalist in my tale, remember to invite everybody—the poor, the hoboes, the junkies, the scumbags on the streets, goddam filthy immigrants, crapartists of every colour, journalists, hustlers, the blind, the lame and the maimed. Do it this way 'cause they can never invite you back.'

He was quick with the paradox and the quip when people tried to heckle him although the did lose his cool once or twice and fell back on calling people who didn't fancy his stories 'hypocrites' and 'shitehawks'. Maybe it was because of this that people began to get a bit cheesed off. Or maybe it was the sheer banality of weighty statements like 'Look, peace is inside you and peace is outside you' or stories that said you should be happy with whatever miserable pittance a boss gave you. More than that, however, it was maybe just that fashions change and maybe he began to run out of stories.

In his latter years when he would start on some yarn some wag would shout 'Heard it before!' from the street corner, or murmers of 'Boring, boring,' would come from those who expected more, or 'Why don't you tell us a true story, about real life?' from those who didn't like folklore. There was also a rumour that all the storytellers were to be banished as they were not conducive to good citizenship and that society needed skills that were really useful and practical and economically relevant and market-driven.

Nobody was too surprised when his body was

discovered in the hills above the city. It only made a brief mention in the evening papers because of the grass and pebbles that were stuffed in his mouth as if somebody was making the point that he should be shut up.

The funny thing was that people began telling his stories again shortly after his murder. Somebody said it was a good career move. And others began to make up stories about him. And others began to make up stories about the stories. And yet others a commentary on the stories. And yet others again an exegesis of the commentary on the stories. And later an explanation of the exegesis of the commentary on the stories. And then an analysis of the explanation of the exegesis of the commentary on the stories. And then a critique of the analysis of the explanation of the exegesis of the commentary on the stories.

And then somebody remembered that the storyteller himself once said, 'Look, a story is just like a mustard seed ... '

The Third World

THERE WAS A RICH MAN AND a poor man. The poor man had to carry the rich man around on his back. They went here, there, and everywhere. They went up hill and down dale. They met Tom, Dick and Harry and Rotschilds and Rockerfellers and O'Reillys. The poor man slept in the cardboard city created by the rich and the rich man slept in the glitzy hotel built by the poor. But every morning the same sun shone on the rich man's face and on the poor man's bum.

The rich man dug his heels into the poor man's neck in order to feel more comfortable. The poor man wrapped the rich man's ankles around his chest in order to feel more safe.

Whenever they saw anything valuable or useful on their journey around the world—food or jewels or oil or riches or minerals or fish—the rich man would kindly ask, 'Hey, why don't you pick that up and I will carry it for you?'

Adam's Story

WHEN ADAM WAS NINE HUNDRED AND twenty years of age, or thereabouts, it dawned on him that his eyes were growing weaker, his voice was failing, his bones were creaking and arthritis was setting in to his joints. He began to notice that the birds of the air died, and the beasts of the field, and every living thing that walked upon the earth. And he thought that such a death might come his way also.

His children often came to visit him, and their children, and their children's children, and their seed and breed and generations. There was nothing he enjoyed more than telling them stories, because stories at that time were young and new and had not been heard before.

'The one about the snake, tell us that one,' said Tufit, who was a bit of a hard man, 'I always liked that one.'

'No. Something more personal,' said Ruthy, 'like the way you met your wife, how it was for you, the first time ever, and that kind of stuff. I have to hear this again.'

'Forget it,' said Harum, 'the one about the apple. I want the apple!'

'It wasn't an apple anyway, you twit. It was a pear.'

'An orange!'

'A fig!'

'A pomegranate!'

Adam had forgotten the details by now it was such a long time ago, and he nearly believed his own version. But there was one thing he hadn't forgotten and it welled up in him like a lump in his throat. He had to get it off his chest to set the record straight.

'Look,' he said, 'it was like this. There was no apple. In fact, there was no fruit at all. Well, of course, there were olives and cherries and berries and lemons and grapefruit and plums and nuts and bananas and growths for which we have no name yet. But none of them were forbidden. There was no forbidden fruit. We could eat them all ... '

There was a great silence that was only broken by a groan from far off which was like unto a myth slowly dying.

'And the tree in the middle of the garden?' asked somebody tentatively.

'There were many trees in the middle of the garden, wherever that was.'

'And the snake?' someone else tried.

'No snake either. Or if there was it was just as friendly as every other animal.'

'And God?'

'He never chucked us out of the Garden. We left ourselves voluntarily.'

Some of the older offspring began to get a little angry, not just because they had had to swallow this stuff for hundreds of years, but because they had to earn their bread by the sweat of their brow. They looked down at their calloused hands, and at the scars and cracks and warts and weals, and they felt more deeply the pain in their lower backs.

'OK, let's get this straight, once and for all,' said Aleymbibic, who appeared already to have the makings of a good committee chairman. 'Do I take it that what you are saying is that yourself and our greatgreatgreatgreatgreat etc grandmother were living together in this fabulous garden, that you had sweet fanny adam to do except to frolick beneath the trees, no stroke of work to do, food and sweet sustenance dripping from the trees, the beasts of the world as your slaves and servants—and then one fine day you just upped and fucked off out of Paradise leaving it all behind you?'

'That's about it in one go,' said Adam, with a certain relief now that the truth was out.

'And why were you so dumbassed stupid, to leave the Garden of Paradise, to leave all that behind you?' asked most of them in chorus.

'Because it was boring, of course,' said Adam, 'boring, boring, boring.'

Ears

THERE WAS A SOLDIER WHO FOUGHT in the great wars in defence of civilisation and democracy who sent the ears of his dead enemies home to his friends.

They thought they were dried apricots because they were a bright yellow and orange colour.

They ate them.

They were, depend upon it, disgusted and horrified and more than even concerned when they learned the truth. This is because they were, after all, nice white people with a good clean liberal conscience.

That did not mean, however, that they did not enjoy them nor find them exceedingly delicious.

An Old Soldier's Recollections

'O, YES, I REMEMBER IT WELL. How could I forget? I learned my trade from this carpenter guy out in the backwoods. He couldn't speak much of my language, but jabbered away nonetheless. I picked up enough of his, enough to understand his instructions. I have to say that he was kind, though. His smile was the better part of him. His wife was a lot quieter, but delivered the goods. Tea and sandwiches and a mug of hot cocoa when it was needed in the long nights after sawing. My experience of carpenters is that they were a rough crew. Great dirty talk and filthy jokes. I suppose that's why I joined the army anyway. I was only doing my duty. Even if I was taking the king's shilling, so what? You must make a living, you know? It's just life, idn't it? That's how it goes. Anyway, this guy was a nice bloke. Paid over the top too. I'm not sure his son approved of me, or even of him. Heard them arguing one night. The lad said that a deal was a deal, and that I shouldn't be given any tips. The apprentice is worthy of his hire, but that's all. The dad just laughed and continued his planing. I sometimes think he thought that the lad was getting too big for his boots. The lad was very slick with his tongue and turned a good yarn. He was also good with the tools.

He had a sure touch and was as deft with his hands as he was with his talk. I often wondered what happened to him? I wouldn't be surprised if he was a master craftsman. He might even be some kind of a scholar earning a fat salary in some college or other. His mother always thought he would come to a sticky end, but she was kinda resigned to it. But the dad, he was the real master craftsman. Made chairs an emperor could sit on. Did a fancy pulpit for the church. Loved his wood the way a poet loves his words, or a soldier his sword. But he was also so practical. 'Fancy works never buttered no parsnips', he would say, and went on to the cold business of making a living. I will always remember him and treasure his advice. 'Keep a firm grip on the plank, and keep the bloody wood straight,' he would say to me, 'and remember that the elm is split with a wedge of its own timber.' I hadn't the least clue as to what that meant, but I took to heart his other advice. Like, he was almost a genius with a few nails. He banged them home straight and true. I always tried to follow his advice when I was hammering nails into the palms of the criminals, and the lowlife forms, and the riffraff, and the subhuman shitebags that we had to nail to the cross. I was always grateful for that. How could I forget? O, yes, I remember him well.'

Another Way

WHEN THE WISE MEN LEFT THE stable they knew they had a problem. They had promised Herod they would go back to his palace and tell him what they had seen, and where he would find the baby king. They had given him their word, and yet they felt their word was not good enough. There was something in his sincere smile, in the whiteness of his teeth, in the firm clasp of his hand, in his direct look into their eyes, in his unfailing courtesy, there was something in his entirely plausible manner that made them hesitate.

'We're in a hurry, anyway,' said the Brown One, 'I don't think there's much good in hanging around. I think we should get out of here fast.'

'Can't agree at all,' said the Yellow Wise Person, 'we must of course keep our word even though the sky fall in. We must tell him about the baby.'

'God will provide,' said the Bronze sage, 'remember we did promise honesty, openness and transparency. We can't escape duty. Duty is paramount. I just don't know what the problem is.'

'The problem is,' said the Dark wise man, 'that we have a feeling that we shouldn't put our trust in princes, that, as we say now, he had an agenda, that what we saw isn't what we got, that he was, as they say, having us on.'

'But it is said that a prince's word is his bond,' said the Bronze one in reply, 'why should we doubt a prince's word?'

'Just because he is a Prince,' said the Brown one, packing his bags, 'we should doubt a prince's word just precisely because he is a prince. He may be a man but a prince is a prince for all that.'

'And anyway there was yer man,' said the Black wise man, who never said much because it was thought that he never had much to say, 'the guy in white with the funny shoulders and the pale face and the thin voice.'

'So what?' said Bronzy, 'he didn't give any reason. Besides we might get lost. Remember we had a star to guide us on the way here. That star has gone down, or on to the west. We need to do what we know. We need to obey the king. We need to keep our word.'

'All he said was that we should go back another way,' said the Wise One with the ruddy complexion, 'who does he think he is, some kind of cartogropher?'

'I think you miss the point,' said the Black one from the south, the one who never said much because he had little enough to say, 'just remember what we saw. Just remember the gifts we brought, the hard coming we had of it. All he told us was that we should go back another way. Wasn't that why we came here? If we didn't come here to go back another way, then what was it all about?'

The Bird and The Maggot

THERE WAS A MAGGOT WHO CRAWLED upon the ground, and sometimes beneath it. He never raised his head because he didn't have to. He preferred digging and grubbing and enjoying the warm feeling as he slithered down and in. Once or twice he had climbed up on a green leaf but had got dizzy and quickly returned to the good earth.

A proud bird landed next to him. His belly was full and he didn't feel like any more maggots that day.

'Listen to me you low-down slithering slimeball,' he said to the maggot. 'I pity you. What a boring life you lead. I can fly anywhere I like. I see the cities of the world. Toledo today and Tenerife tomorrow. I can deliver messages from the good and the great around the globe. One of my kind gives inspiration to poets, and yet another descended on the apostles. We provide music for lovers. We herald the beginning of spring. I'm free to do whatever I like and to see whatever I will. What will you have done when your time is up?'

The maggot didn't particularly wish to get involved in this debate, unaccustomed as he was. He also knew that his own gruff voice could never match the silver tones of the bird.

'And what will you have seen, ha?' asked the bird, getting even closer.

'The ground, I'll have seen the ground,' said the maggot somewhat impatiently.

The bird burst into a guffaw of laughter scattering feathers all around with sheer mirth. 'Seven inches a day!' he jeered, 'I travel through the air more in three seconds than you do upon the ground in three years. You'll have seen the ground! You'll have seen the ground! What a laugh!'

'But I will,' said the maggot, 'and I will have left my mark upon it.'

The Last Butterfly

IT WAS MY LAST SUMMER BEFORE I went to secondary school. If it wasn't, it was certainly the last summer I spent with my brother as the following year he went off to work in Tramore on the roundabouts. We were staying with my aunt at Coolfeakle and she was as changeable as the clouds. But she did let us wander at will through the fields and meadows as long as we fetched water from the well. I thought she kept a cobweb on her head until Martin told me it was a hairnet she wore to keep her hair from going grey. I never knew when he was joking me or not.

We had picked mushrooms in the morning because it had been damp, and Auntie fried them with buttered potatoes and cabbage for dinner. They were things I would never eat at home but hours rambling through the fields with the wind at my back and the grass under my feet would give you an appetite for old boots. The sun came out while we ate and I could see Auntie smile at it as if she knew something that it did not.

'Not before time, either,' she said, as she shuffled back to the dresser for a side plate.

'I suppose it'll shine all the time after tomorrow,' Martin said. 'Just after we get the train.'

'And it'll blaze when we go back to school,' I chimed in, showing I could be as pessimistic as the rest.

'Don't moan,' Auntie said, but not severely. 'Moaning never stopped the rain. Did you never hear that?'

We didn't answer as we didn't want another long gabble about the weather. It amazed me how grown-ups could go on and on and on about the weather as if it really mattered. My motto was if you didn't like the weather just wait a while and it would change.

'I think I'll catch ladybirds,' I said after we had put our dishes in the basin, but I didn't get any great response from Martin.

He came with me nonetheless. We went through the Potter's field and up past the Bracken Glen and round by Maggie Maurice's old house which was now deserted since she was taken away and out as far as Aughinish. We could see the sea from there sucking the gentle heat from the sun and rolling round the rocks to the shore. I hadn't caught any ladybirds yet but I still had my jam-jar.

A fly went by with a hum in it but who wants to catch a fly? Martin said, 'This is boring.'

I didn't think so because I liked the sea and the sky and the green fields that were everywhere and laid themselves out in all directions. Sometimes I wished I could just run and run and run away over the horizon and throw kisses at the wheat and the corn and smell everything as it is first thing in the morning. There were times when I would love to be a scarecrow but that was a secret I would never tell anybody.

'Look, look at them,' Martin said, grabbing me by the arm and pointing my eyes towards Muckers' Acre.

I didn't see anything unusual but Martin seemed intent on showing me anyway. There was the field and some haystacks and a man and another person near the gate. He was wearing a bright red and yellow anorak which reminded me of fried eggs and tomato ketchup. His size shadowed the other person and it wasn't until they began to climb over the gate that I saw it was a woman. She wore a green headscarf the colour of cooking apples of the kind that are too bitter for even Auntie's tarts.

'Come on, let's follow them,' Martin said.

'What for?'

'It might be fun.'

'I want to collect ladybirds.'

'You're a cissy.'

'You're silly.'

'Maybe they're spies.'

'There's nothing round here to spy on.'

'Oh yes there is. The Relihan's house was broken into last week and they know it was sussed out first. I bet you that's what they're up to. Why else would they be going through the fields and not round by the road?'

I couldn't answer that so I tagged on behind. Martin kicked the thistles as if they were footballs but I preferred to leave them standing. Anyway, most of them just jumped back up as if he was wasting his time. I thought time was there to be wasted but Martin was the one who always wanted to be doing something. We stayed at least a field behind and they were making very slow progress. Maybe they were noticing everything like Martin said as spies and robbers have to notice everything. We also had to stay out of sight and picked and ate some blackberries from the bushes. I wouldn't let him use my jar to collect them as I detested blackberry jam and I knew what I wanted it for.

'Think Auntie will kill us if we come home with our feet wet?' I asked, as we were going through a soggy dip towards a stream.

'Who cares?' Martin said. 'We're going home tomorrow. Ma won't mind. She'll be washing all our clothes anyhow.'

'I like it here,' I said. 'I think I'd like to live in the country when I grow up. It's big. It's wild.'

'It's boring.'

Martin thought everything was boring apart from his crummy records. He'd listen to the same song for hours and discuss it with his pals. I think Ma sent him down the country just for a bit of peace.

We were trailing along beside the stream on the way to Berwick's Wood when I saw it.

It floated out from underneath a tall fern and moved on to a ray of sunlight. It had the most beautiful black wings I had ever seen and they were tinged with red like jam through a doughnut.

I could not tell one kind of butterfly from another but I knew that this one was special. It flitted in and out of the sunlight as if it was preening itself and more than anything else in the world I just wanted to stay in that spot and admire it.

'Look, Martin! Look!' I whispered, fearing that any loud voice would frighten it away.

Martin looked back and cast one eye on it. 'Yes, it's a butterfly or a moth or something. It's lovely. Now come on.'

'Just a minute,' I said, 'I want to look at it.'

It moved across the stream as if on a ferry of sundust and

just as I was about to wave it goodbye it alighted on a thin reed which jutted out from the bank. It appeared even more beautiful when at rest and I stepped out onto the stones to get a closer look.

I could not believe my luck when it didn't fly away. I stretched out my hand breathlessly and yet it did not move. The black was lovely, lovely like the mouth of a cave and the red was as the dawn coming through it. I could have prayed that it would never move and that I could stay there watching it more beautiful than all its surroundings for ever.

I heard Martin shouting at me from up the stream. He seemed miles away but somehow I didn't care. He shouted again more angrily this time and I knew I would have to leave. Quickly, without thinking I stretched out the jam-jar and enclosed my butterfly under the lid. Thankfully he could make no sound as I did not wish to hurt it in any way and I knew that I would soon let it go.

'Hurry up! What's keeping you? We've lost them.'

I tried to show him my black beauty but he wasn't interested. He just kept pushing ahead through the scrub and yapping at me to move it.

'Damn it,' he said as our rough path forked out from the edge of the stream towards the wood. 'Because of you we'll never know which way they went. You've blown it.'

'Maybe they left a clue,' I said, hoping I might have said the right thing. 'Maybe we'll find a piece of cloth on a bush.'

'Rubbish,' he said, pushing ahead. 'We'll just have to go one way and take a chance we're right.'

I followed him faithfully through the wood even

pretending to hide behind the same trees as he did. Every so often I got a chance to look at my butterfly and he would gently flit his wings at me. The brambles that coiled out to ambush us didn't seem to bother Martin and I wouldn't have minded if he didn't let them snap back on me. I don't think he even noticed.

We had been walking up a hill for some time when the trees began to thin out. We came to a barbed wire fence but the path turned and ran along beside it. There were very few trees on the other side of the fence and Martin said we should go through as we would get a better view and might spot them. We moved further along the path to try to find an opening when I saw the green scarf caught on the wire.

'Come on,' Martin urged, and I went through first and then held the wire up for him as he was bigger.

We ran along the grass margin of the trees and then up the hill again as if we were on a murder hunt. I'm not sure where we went after that as I just followed Martin as he ran and crouched and zig-zagged and ducked through ferns and bushes until we came to the lane.

'I hope this leads on to the road,' I said. 'I'm tired.'

'Come on,' he said, and I followed.

The lane ran right up to a high wall with a big wooden door cold in the middle. It was closed. We pushed but it would not open.

'What do we do now,' I said, 'go all the way back?'

'Give me a leg up,' Martin said, as he tried to get a foothold in the wall. I helped him and he managed to hoist himself up far enough to see over.

'What is it?' I asked, 'What's there?'

'Nothing much only another big field.'

'Well come on then.'

'Just a minute. I'll be down in a minute.'

'Give me a hand up so.'

'There's no need. It's nothing. Just a field.'

'Must be a great view if you ask me.'

When he did come down I thought he was angry with me. He said nothing for a while but just strode away back towards the hill which seemed much higher now. I found it more difficult to keep up with him this time and I knew it was a long way home.

'What's that you have in the jar?' he asked, suddenly.

'It's my butterfly,' I said. 'Don't you remember?'

'Show it to me.'

He glanced at it briefly and what looked like a smile appeared on his lips.

'Silly girlish stuff,' he sneered, as he opened the jam-jar and rolled my beautiful black butterfly between the palms of his hands.

All I ever remembered then was the black powder falling and the fleck of red on his fingernails.

The Only True Reason Why Cain Killed His Brother Abel

ONE EVENING WHEN ABEL WAS ABOUT to go out do a dance he came down the stairs. Cain was sitting at the table scratching his locks and generally minding his own business.

'What's up? Where are you going?' he asked, for the sake of saying something or anything at all.

'It's none of your fuckin' business,' Abel said, trying to prevent his nose from taking off into the air. 'Who the fuck are you you fuckin' fucker for askin' me where the fuck am I goin'. And as I'm at it why the fuck are you wearin' my fuckin' purple fuckin' polka dot tie?'

'Because, it was lying in the heap on the floor through which you jump every morning. You missed it and I thought as you weren't wearing it it would be perhaps alright or even ok.'

'Well it's not fuckin' ok and didn't I tell you not to lay a fuckin' hand on any fuckin' thing belongin' to me afuckingen?'

'Well, you did, of course, but so what and what is that to me? It's not as if you are going to do anything about it, is it, now?'

Cain reached for the big bread knife on the kitchen

table and without pausing to adjust his aim stuck it viciously into his brother's neck. He made sure that he would never wear his purple polka dot tie again as he slashed it through the middle as he pulled the knife out of his throat. It was covered in blood anyway.

Chaos Theory

THE WOMAN LIVED IN THE BIG city with her lovely family and devoted husband. She was very religious and lit the brightly-coloured candles and prayed at the correct shrines. She paid her dues and lowered her eyes and covered her head. Her faith was as deep as the earth and as firm as the foundations on which the city was built.

Some charlatans who had often predicted the end of the world also predicted the earthquake. In the former they were so far wrong but in the latter they were absolutely correct.

The city was devastated in seven seconds flat. Bridges buckled and buildings collapsed without warning. The earth opened and swallowed up thousands. Thousands more were crushed under flats and offices and houses. Thousands more again just vanished never to be heard of by the few who remained.

By some fortune or happenstance the good woman survived under two beams of wood which marked an *x* over her head. Her lovely family and devoted husband were not so lucky meeting various sticky and gruesome ends which are too awful to recount.

It wasn't then that her faith was crushed just like her lovely family and devoted husband or that it vanished like the thousands who were swallowed up in the cracks of the earth, it was more that it was shaken like the foundations of the city which a few seconds before seemed so secure. And it being shaken she required answers.

She betook herself to her religious advisor and sought from him the final and ultimate answer as to why her city had been destroyed and her family killed. He told her it was the will of God. 'Who knows,' he said, 'maybe something worse would have happened if it had not been for this.'

She was puzzled at these words being a simple but good woman as she didn't know how God could have willed the destruction of her lovely family and devoted husband, and even more so it puzzled her that anything worse could have happened than the earthquake which devastated her city. So she went on her way perplexed and dismayed.

She then went to her ministering priest who told her it was a punishment for all of their sins. But she was puzzled at these words because she knew she hadn't sinned since she knew the meaning of the word and likewise she knew her family and friends to be righteous and proper and good-living and God-fearing. So she continued on her way still perplexed and dismayed.

She then met a guru with a long beard who had studied the latest physics at the cuboid glass-covered state-of-the-art university (now demolished) at the edge of the city.

'You want to know the reason for this earthquake?' he asked, 'The real and ultimate reason and not something about faults in the earth's plates?'

'Yes,' she said, 'I want to know why.'

'The reason for the earthquake which demolished our city,' he said, 'is because an ant farted in Tierra del Fuego.'

Charity

A LONG TIME AGO IN THOSE DARK ages before the torch of enlightenment lit up the world the rule of life was very simple. That rule was: 'No work—no food.' It may just as well have said: 'If you don't work, you will die like a dog.'

This was a rule that was inculcated into the child in the cradle and the innocent in school and the pensioner in front of the box. If a doubt was raised, here, there, or anywhere in any household whatsoever, you can be sure that the wagging finger spake: 'If you don't work, you will die of hunger!'

Therefore, and without doubt, there were no dossers or shirkers or lazy bones around. Neither were there tramps or tinkers or beggars, or people with only one leg, or one hand, or one eye. And therefore little need for taxes or rates or social welfare. And people were happy because what they earned they owned, and nobody's hand was in their pocket except their own.

But one day a stubborn pig-headed type said to himself: 'Fuck this for a lark! Why all this sweat and toil when I don't even have time to drink the fruit of my labour?' And he sank down on the road beside the bridge to wait for death.

And the people came and mocked and jeered at him, and they even started taking bets as to when exactly he would die. But when he wasn't fading away or obviously dying it dawned on them that someone was bringing him food or sustenance without their knowledge.

And they hid in the shadows and waited through the night. And when they saw a small boy bringing him a crust of bread just before dawn, they jumped on him and started kicking him and thumping him about the head.

'Just who do you think you are?' they screamed, as the poison and hate curdled along their tongues. 'Don't you know that you are encouraging laziness? Don't you know that you are bringing laziness into the world? Laziness! Laziness! Laziness! Laziness!'

'Is that the same word for charity?' asked the child.

The Confession Box

THERE WAS THIS WOMAN WHO WENT unto the priest in confession. She wanted advice rather than forgiveness.

'My husband's the problem,' she said. 'He hits me. He beats the shite out of me. He gives me no money. He comes in pissed and totally langers. He doesn't give two fucks about the kids. He doesn't know them. Worse than that he's unfaithful. And he won't speak to me about our problems. I'll speak to him. When I speak to him and tell him what's wrong with him he shuts up. It's as if he doesn't want to hear me. What am I supposed to do?'

'I haven't a clue,' said the priest, 'not the faintest.'

'He won't even read Maureen Gaffney,' she said.

'He's not the only man,' said the priest, wrapping his black robes around him for protection.

'But I came to you,' she said, she said, 'because you are learned and educated. You have written books. You do the premarriage courses in the parish. And now you have the neck to tell me you don't have any advice?'

'I'm sorry,' said the priest, 'I'm really sorry,' from out of the darkness,' 'but I'm afraid you have fogotten just one thing, one important thing. There is one good reason why I never will be able to give you advice.'

'And what's that?' she said, with some hope, as we all do.

'I was married myself once,' he said, and closed the shutter.

A Cure for Love

THIS POOR UNFORTUNATE WAS IN LOVE. He knew this because his hands were shaking and his knees were weak and he couldn't seem to stand on his own two feet. The woman knew this also, as women do, but her heart was as cold as the grave, or else she was in love with someone else. One way or the other, she more or less disdainfully ignored him, or would merely deign to allow her left earlobe incline in his direction.

'Patience, time and tide and space and distance,' his friends would tell him, because most of them had been through this particular mill, as men do.

He wrote to an agony aunt but she wasn't much better.

'How can I express my love for her?' he had asked, hoping for a clear answer.

'It doesn't matter how you express it,' she replied, 'so long as you practice safe sex. You can't be too careful these days.'

'And how should I approach her?' he had asked, hoping for some useful advice.

'The most common way is from the front,' she replied, 'but there are many books which suggest alternatives.'

'You could, of course, kill yourself,' suggested a friend,

who although he was happily married had failed in his attempts three times.

In the end he decided to go to Dr. Psycho who knew all the answers.

'O, doctor, I'm in trouble,' he said, and poured forth his story.

'Well, yes,' said Dr. Psycho, after he had listened to him several times and walked around the table, 'I recognise the symptoms all right—a racing pulse, dizziness in the head, music in the ears, a pale face, a faraway look in the eyes, trembling fingers—I have no doubt that you are suffering from TOAFULS, or totally obsessed and fucked-up love syndrome.'

'But what's the cure?' he begged, 'what am I to do?'

'I'll tell you what you'll do,' said Psycho in measured and professional tones. 'Get up and go out of this office. Find a white cat who has a wart on his tail. Cut it out with a blackthorn knife. Cut it exactly into two halves and sprinkle it with the juice of a newt's eye and the jam of a frog's toe. Boil it slowly in an oyster shell which has been salvaged from a rusty wreck in the Straights of Gibraltar. Go out to a hazel wood when a fire is in your head. Eat one half slowly chewing it on the right hand side of your mouth only, then throw the other over your left shoulder in a north-westerly direction just as the sun is going down. Then, run home as fast as your legs will carry you and bury your head beneath the blankets.'

He was listening carefully to Psycho all this time, listening to his smooth calm professional voice, and his reassuring tones.

'And are you telling me that this will cure my love-sickness?' he asked, between hope and credulity.

'Well, I'm not saying it will cure it precisely,' said the doctor, 'but it will do as much good as anything else you try.'

The Gorilla's Armpit

'IS A GARBAGE CAN ANY MORE real than Buckingham Palace?' Cary Grant is reported to have asked once without waiting for the answer from the fairy princess or the hobbledehoy at the end of the street.

He may have been right too for all I know since it was not the kind of question which I was, as they say nowadays, into.

I preferred the simpler questions which my slide of hand or rule of thumb could manage and the even simpler answers which could be swallowed at a price.

And as one swallow doesn't make a summer I wasn't too cheesed off when the knock came even if it did force me momentarily away from my sesame and chick-pea dip. I supposed it might even be Molly Coddle again with yet another inquiry about the bruise marks on her thigh.

'I'm a psychoanalyst or something,' I was fed up telling her, 'not a psychometrician', but my measured tones were usually lost on her.

'I have to talk to you,' the weedy little squeak at the door pipped up at me after I had loosened the chains, undid the bolts, turned off the alarm and switched on the video.

'*Have* is a big word,' I said. 'Do you mean *have* as in

possession, proprietorship, a bird in the hand or have as in essential, necessitous, what makes the old wife trot or what? And do you have any money? Have in this case as *in sine qua non* or nothing.'

'I have to talk to you,' he said again, same tone, same voice, same earnestness. 'You may even find it interesting.'

'Yes, but does it pay?' I insisted, 'That is the only interest that interests me whether it be simple or compound.'

'O, I think this will compound you beyond your wildest dreams,' he said, allowing himself a nailparing of a smile which was tinged with worry and laced with excitement.

'Has your boyfriend left you?' I ventured as we went through the hall hoping I might at least detect what colour of beast I was dealing with. He knew when he was being baited and said nothing apart from making the odd gurgle which might have been addressed to the mooses on the wall.

'Is it your dreams?' I said. 'If they are colourless and green and sleep furiously then we have a deep structure which has only been rarely observed.'

'Agh!' he grunted in a couple of languages and waved the back of his hand as if he was brushing dandruff off a moonbeam.

'Then you must have joined a political party and can't sleep at night. It's more common than you think. In which case I can't do anything for you but I know a publican who can.'

'It's not that,' he said, 'it's this.'

'If it's not one thing it's always the other,' I said, sounding very philosophical and showing that I knew something about the law of the excluded middle even at meal times.

We were now in my room which had the usual prerequisites of such a room which are familiar to all who either have an imagination, a memory, a great-grandaunt or have been to the cinema.

I went to my big desk and sheltered myself behind it. Professional etiquette demands that there be a distance between the curer and the cured. It also put me at an advantage.

'Name?' I asked, taking out a new fat file.

'It's not important,' he said, 'it's what you are.'

'Or the way you tell them,' I said, 'but I can't proceed unless I have a name. Any dream will do but first we must have the naming of parts. So, what'll it be then?'

'Val,' he said as if he was ashamed of it, 'Val Kyrie.'

'Well bless the Lord,' I said, 'have you been marching long?'

'All the way,' he said, 'from the top of the morning to the ends of the earth.'

'So it shows. But what was it you said you wanted? You want to sing like Gigli?'

'That's not a priority,' he said, shuffling around in his seat as if he had a bee in his bum. He produced a small black box from beneath his cloak and plonked it on my desk.

'It is this,' he said, 'not that. It's not what you think.'

'I don't think,' I said, feeling insulted, 'I analyse.'

'That's just it,' he shot in, 'I want this analysed.'

'Depends what it is,' I said, opening my drawer and looking for my price list. 'If it's a rat you shouldn't come to me. You should see a psychologist. If it's a rabbit you should see a conjuror. If it's a red herring you should see a priest. If it's a white elephant you should see the minister concerned. If it's a sacred cow you should see the butcher. If it's a tailor's goose you should see a taxidermist. If it's a bat from your belfry I might be able to do something for you but only if the timing is right.'

'I don't know what it is,' he said, matter-of-factly like, as if he was saying 'It's a nice day' or 'How's your father?' or 'You don't close your eyes any more when I kiss your lips.'

'In that case we ought to have a look, oughtn't we?' I said, conscious of the time factor always, and especially how time is money, how it flies, how it cures all things, how it subdues all things, how it will abide no man, how it reveals all secrets, how it has a taming hand, how it is the nurse and breeder of all good, how it is the best doctor, how with it even a bear can be taught to dance, how it should be taken by the forelock, how all the treasures of the earth cannot bring it back, how it leaves its shadow behind, is the gentle deity, does not bow to you, is the herald of truth, is the one loan that no one can repay, makes hay, works wonders and is man's equal.

I stretched out to open the box but he jumped up and stayed my hand.

'Are you sure you want me to do this?' I asked, as I was never that tolerant with nervous patients or their arts.

'Of course,' he remonstrated, if that locution is still in use, 'it's just that I would like to have it opened under laboratory conditions.'

'No problem,' I said, lifting it up carefully and bringing it over to my thingubator on the other side of the room.

'This is my laboratory and these are my conditions so I take it we are fulfilled.'

'It will have to do,' he said, not appearing at all satisfied, 'it's just that I don't want it to escape. If it escapes it would be a disaster.'

'Hold on,' I said, getting wary, 'if it's the cobalt A-bomb in embryo or something you can puff off. I have my standards, you know. I'm not just a pretty face and don't fancy being used. I may be Dr. Shekel to you but I'm not Mr. Hydrogen to anybody, not even myself.'

'It's not dangerous,' he insisted, 'it's just that it's my life's work and I couldn't bear to see it lost.'

'Don't worry,' I said, as I didn't have a shoulder to cry on, 'I'm an expert in state-of-the-heart technology so let's take a goosey gander at your little black box and put you out of your misery.'

I laid it carefully in the thingubator and he gave me the key. It was any common or garden shed key which could do the job from either hand, although it was possible to surmise in a case of urgent necessity in dire extremis if both hands and legs were tightly bound by villains or rogues it could work with the mouth on condition that one was possessed of strong teeth or at least firmly secured dentures. It was the kind of key that would be utterly unremarkable if it was thrown in its lot with other knicknacks, whatjamecallits, doodads, bibelots and old nails.

But it did the job.

I prised open the lid and felt his tense hand gripping my arm. His breath smelt of meals of long ago and the warmth of dog fur. I once knew a fellow who lived entirely on catfish chasseur and he was more pleasant company cheek to cheek. But this was his baby so who was I to object? Besides he may have been rich enough to bid for the time of day for all I knew.

'What do you see?' he asked, almost in a panic giving me the benefit of his last crapmeat meal in my ear. 'How do you read it? What's it all about? Can you explain it?'

'I don't know,' I said, 'I don't think I've ever seen it before, but it's not very unusual at the same time.'

'Look carefully,' he pleaded, 'you've got the skills, you're a professional, you know how to see, you're my only chance.'

'I only see what you see,' I said, 'a blob of glob is a blob of glob is a blob of glob.'

There was a bit more to it than that because it was bubbling up and changing its shape even though it was quite cold. There was also a sprinkling of what looked like grey dust unevenly spread here and there.

'Keep looking,' he insisted. 'Analyse, schematize, unscramble, you can do it.'

I did as he said and stared. I had to admit it began to get fascinating as it changed colours and texture and shape before my eyes. It began to resemble for all the world a child's penny kaleidoscope found in a lucky bag and viewed through a crazy mirror. Then it took on the shape of a dome, or perhaps a crystal ball and I thought I began to see the colours clearing, mellowing, becoming more defined.

'Now!' he said, gripping me viciously by the arm and almost thrusting my head into the box, 'now, tell me what you see!' I recoiled violently, screaming and banging my head against the laboratory wall. He told me a long time afterwards that I tried to pluck out my eyes and that I sank my nails into my cheeks. He also told me that I cursed so violently he thought I was speaking in tongues. Apparently I passed out and it took me a long time to recover my power of speech.

'Was it a monster, from some Nazi or other?' I had asked him when I began to come round.

He shook his head.

'An atheist, a communist, an anti-christ?'

He shook his head again.

'A Catholic, a Protestant, a Jain?'

He shook his head once more. There was sorrow in his shake. There may even have been tears in his eyes but I wasn't sure what they meant.

'Tell me what you saw,' he asked calmly but firmly. 'I must know what you saw. You must tell me.'

'Not until you tell me where you got it,' I said, 'I must know too.'

'It was a young girl,' he said, almost wistfully. 'Actually an unborn baby. Stainless. Immaculate. We knew we'd have to abort and she didn't have a chance. I would have saved her if I could but I thought it more important to save her soul. It wasn't difficult to trap the soul now that we have the technology. I just wanted to know what it was really like—under laboratory conditions, scientifically, if you know what I mean.'

'I'll tell you,' I said, 'I'll tell you what I saw. Just remember I warned you.'

A Yarn of Fifty Words Only

A SAINT LIVED A LIFE OF PERFECT holiness. He kept all the eleven commandments.

When he died he was condemned to hell.

'Why?' he asked, bemusedly, 'didn't I do all that was asked?'

'O, yes, you did, and more,' said Peter, 'but didn't you hear that we changed the rules?'

The Bishop Who Stuck His Finger In The Dyke

'COME QUICKLY!' THE BOY SHOUTED IN a panic, 'There's a hole in the dyke and the water's rushing in!'

The bishop sighed at yet another emergency but at least it wasn't anyone crying wolf. He got out of bed, lifted his belly after him, leaned on his crozier, put on his purple robes, wondered why the Galatians never replied to Paul since he had written to them and strolled down to the shore. This time the boy was right. He was a nice boy. He knew he was a nice boy. The water wasn't rushing in, as he said, but there was a hole the size of a wagging finger or a stubby thumb in the dyke, and some water was, indeed, pouring through. It was the sort of pour that would fill a decent wine glass in about seven seconds. And this dyke was the only protection that his flock had against the big bad sea which rocked and rolled all the way to the west.

He stuck his finger in the dyke to stop the flow. As it was not an unpleasant sensation he said to the boy: 'Go thou unto the town and get the workers and the laity and the ordinary people who clean the church and serve the food and till the fields and teach in school and make the children and tell them that God's church doth need them quickly and even pronto.'

The boy did as he was told as he was a good boy and a friend of the bishop's.

Off he went as fast as his legs could carry him as he sure as hell had no other means of transport and left the bishop there with his finger stuck firmly in the dyke. The bishop quickly began to understand that the water was not going to stop that easily as it was now trickling up his wrist, in under his sleeve, travelling inexorably towards his armpit to lodge under the warm hairy hole of his shoulder. Very soon he had to put his two fingers in and this didn't cause him any discomfort either. But he then discovered that his two fingers were widening the fissure rather than solving the problem. With a certain degree of frustration he shoved his whole hand in. He had to push it right up to the hilt and yet they hadn't come.

He dug his crozier deep into the earth for support and then stuck his two hands into the hole which was now like unto a big crack. It made little difference. The sea rushed in over his two hands, then up his neck, then washing his ears, then over his head while down below it was up to his knees. He thought he was done for. Something in the back of his head told him he had once seen a film about the flood, or maybe it was Moses parting the Red Sea with his rod. But just then he saw the boy and the people of the village coming over the haunches of the hill.

They shouted to him. 'Let go! Let it be! There's no use! Get out or you will be drowned!' He thought he heard someone say 'Get the finger out!' but he knew it was unlikely that anyone had a sense of humour at a time like this.

For some reason he obeyed them. It hurt him to have to obey the laity but it was either that or death. The wide sick-slopping sea lapped around his mouth and sucked at his breath.

He let go and was swept with the tide. Down the fields he went and then past the church where he had preached and the village green where he had controlled their play and the parish hall where he had supervised their leisure and through the streets of the town where he had walked in suitable procession. He saw the people out at their doors and at their windows waving to him and shaking their arms.

This cheered him much and he raised his hand to bless them in return.

He didn't realise, however, that they were waving him goodbye.

There Was a Knock on the Door and ...

... A BUNCH OF STUDENTS BARGED IN. Fairly scruffy and ragamuffin as would be expected, but some determination in their stride. Injustice knitting their brows and lips tight with purpose.

'We wish to lodge a complaint,' said their leader. He might have been a nice guy and might yet become a politician.

'And what is it about this time?' asked the weary professor, 'Is it this lecturer guy who insults your non-political non-opinions? Somebody said something that is not relevant to the exams? You have to buy a book? A bad grade incommensurate with your own opinion of yourselves? I'm all ears.'

They had heard this before, of course, but didn't care.

'It's a lot more serious than that.'

'Well, I'm delighted to hear that you student types are getting serious. Are you about to oppose tyranny and imperial aggression? Agitate for an end to third-world debt? Maybe even a little demonstration outside the US embassy that might endanger your summer work visas? A letter to the paper, perhaps?'

'I fully realise,' said their spokesman, 'that you

singlehandedly ended the war in Vietnam, and that you put the fear of God into the authorities with your powerful rhetoric, and that the CIA had put a contract out on you before you went to find yourself in Khatmandu, but I'm afraid that this has to do with the real reason we are here in this university as students—our exams.'

The professor looked at him. A gutsy guy with balls. Somebody who could stand on his two hind legs.

'It's all right for you lot,' he said, trying to scrape for the riposte that would hit home. 'You have only to write the exams, I have to read them.'

He thought for a moment that they had backed off. He'd always known that the flash of a red biro frightened off even the toughest student.

'It's like this,' said the student, as collectedly as he had been from the start. 'There is a thief in the class. He steals our lecture notes, our folders, our files. He may even steal our books. We fear he will pass his exams and get his degree under false pretences. We think he should be disciplined, or even expelled.'

The professor sat back on his chair fully satisfied that this was what a professorial chair was for. A grin spread across his jowls. He snapped the red biro on his teeth and chewed to his satisfaction.

'Pshaw!' he spat across at them. It was a word he had always wanted to use but never had the opportunity until now. 'You lot burst in here telling me that another student is stealing your notes and folders and so on and so on, and you urge me to dump him in some way. Can you be serious? You lot who steal all you know every day from

Baudrillard and Chomsky and Gramsci and Lacan and Jung and Marx and me and Barthes and Eco and Tagliatelli and Kristeva and Cioran and Steiner and Berlin and Hamburger and Freud and Ryle and Dworkin and Klein and Loos and Privi and Bultmann and Verga and Brocoli and Whorf and Truffault and Wajda and Wanker and Tzara and Foucald and Keynes and Kearney and Kiberd and Heyek and Cayek and Buber and Blitzen and Bevis and Buttid and Benjamin—and you have the neck to come in here and ask me to chuck out some poor student you steals from you! Get some sense of proportion! Get a life!'

Flat Earth

IN THOSE FAR OFF DAYS WHEN people were a lot less gullible than they are now some people maintained that the earth was as flat as a billiards table. They said that if you went to the edge of the world you would fall off and go down, down, down—to Hell, maybe, or certainly to the Kingdom of Darkness from which there was no return.

But there were others who said that the world was as round as a ball and that if you walked west you would certainly return from the east, no different from a fly doddling around an apple.

But there were others who said that the world was oval-shaped, but nobody bothered with them as anybody who played with oval balls was *ipso facto* a bit queer.

But those who maintained that the world was flat like a billiard table soon began to fight with those who thought it was round and circular like a ball. And even though there were wise men and elders and even geniuses on each side they could not agree whether the flatters or the ballers were ultimately right as they had no common ground between them.

And because they were people, and because they

couldn't possibly think of any other way of resolving their conflict, and because they were never likely to agree with one another, they decided to finish their dispute by war, because they were, after all, people. And even though cities were razed to the ground and priceless treasures destroyed for ever and countless millions of people annihilated, at least the war came to an end and the question was finally decided.

And the professors and the wise men began to research and to publish their findings of how the world was flat because it was they, the flatearthers, who had won the war.

And just in case there might be any different or dissenting opinion they collected all their enemies together, or those that were left of them, and they bundled them into cars and carriages and chariots. And then they drove the cars and the carriages and the chariots over the cliff at the edge of the world, because after all, they were right.

The Flowers And The Weeds

THE GARDEN OF THE KING WAS beautiful and neat and grand. Lawns as smooth as silk stretching down to the river. Flowerbeds in all their glory as far as the eye could see. Statues of princes and of gods here and there exposing their beauty to the birds.

The flowers were proud of themselves because they were given especial attention. They were fed with the best fertilizer when they were hungry, and were cooled with the coolest water in the heat of midsummer. The royal gardeners came to speak to them and to praise them for their beauty, and the princess would kiss them when she was lonely.

'Humph!' the flowers would say to the weeds, 'you shouldn't be here at all. You are dirty and rough and ugly and common. Most of you don't even have a name. And, what's more, you stink.'

And the weeds would hide far away for shame behind the shade of the tree in the corner of the garden beside the fence.

'The princess was here this morning,' said the flowers haughtily, 'and she bent down and inhaled our fragrance, and she now carries our sweetness around on her royal person. She couldn't even be bothered trampling you lot down. You're not worth it!'

But they didn't know that the princess was shortly to be married off to a prince who was as ugly as a frog, had the manners of a pig, was as thick as two planks and had ears like jug-handles. But he was a prince and they would have to have a royal wedding to satisfy the tabloid newspapers and give the workers a few hours off.

So the royal gardener went forth into the garden and plucked the beautiful flowers that smelled so sweetly. And they were laid in the cathedral, and strewn under the wheels of the carriage, and put into the hands of the footmen and flunkeys, and into the hair of the princess, and special fat purple gaudy ones for the lapel of the prince to distract attention from his ears.

And the weeds in the shade of tree at the back of the garden beside the fence in the corner of the royal place were completely forgotten. They could not take part in this great celebration because they still had their heads on.

As It is in Heaven

SHE DIED AND WENT TO HEAVEN. Peter was delighted at those pearly gates because they hadn't let a woman in for some time. And she was delighted herself because there wasn't much housework to be done. The angels did most of it.

She was thrilled and literally over the moon to be introduced to God for the first time. He was friendly and courteous and kind and had a gleam in his eye behind the bushy brows.

And she was even more thrilled when he took her into his private suite to show her his etchings, as he said. He dismissed the angelic guard and sat her down.

They spent some time talking about this and that and then he put his hand on her knee.

'What do you think you're doing?' she asked, her voice all aquiver with horror and delight and disgust and surprise.

'What do you think I am doing?' he said, as he moved his hand further up her thigh. 'Weren't you alive once?'

'But why?' she pleaded, 'Why? Why? Why?'

'Because that's the way it is,' he said, plainly enjoying himself, 'that's just the way it is. Or didn't you know that?'

'I swear I didn't,' she said, 'honest to God.'

'Well then,' he said, 'I obviously didn't give you lot enough brains.'

Heresies

THE JOKER WAS DYING. HE HAD spent his life joking and jeering and mocking and taking the piss and sending up the dour doughnuts of humanity. In truth, he had often thrown the facile water of levity on deep-down serious subjects. Some of those subjects were so serious that they could not be broached without searing pain and soul-raking angst.

His relations gathered around his death-bed, and even his friends (at least some of them), and his acquaintances, and those who had a grin on their chins and a glint in their eyes even though they did their best to hide it.

If he thought that life was a joke, that was not what life thought about him. That was why Death was sent and hovered over his bed.

His friends and relations were dressed in clothes as black as Mrs. Kennedy's, and so was Death. You would hardly recognise one rather than the other. Some were weeping, and some were keening, and some were mashing their teeth.

'Holy shit,' he said, 'what's up with you?' It looked as if he was getting peeved with them despite the glint in his own eye. 'You look like a shower of moaning mollies and weeping willies. Faces as long as a dark wet night in Two Mile Boris without a bottle of whiskey. You'd think you'd think that the likes of me would never be here again. Cheer up, for God's sake!'

'But we are thinking of God,' they said, 'something you never did during your life. That's what bothers us.'

'That's where you're mistaken,' he said in his weak voice, a voice over which funny shadows still flitted. 'A day never passed without my thanking God profusely for the many gifts he gave me. Some people are called to prayer. I was called to mockery. It's as simple as that.'

'But that's not what the priests say.'

'If the priests are so sure of God's grace and blessing, why are they all so miserable, and stuck in the mud?'

If there was a priest in the room he retreated quietly into the corner along with Death.

'Listen,' said the joker, 'this is how I see it. God is not too far away now. I hear the beating of his angels' wings already. He'll be in through the window or down the chimney any minute now. And if he sees you (let's suppose for the moment that he is a man) gathered around me as dour as boors, as weepy as grey rain on the mountain, as miserable as misery, he will inevitably conclude that I am a dull bollucks myself, a real serious fart, a pussy person, and that I have not been true to myself. In that case he will send me to Hell. So cheer up! Be of good heart! Put on a happy face! I want to go to Heaven. It's up to you ... '

They weren't sure, of course, whether he was joking or serious.

Jesus Wept

AND IT CAME TO PASS IN those days that Jesus was born in Bethlehem of Judea to Mary, and to Joseph the woodworker. And after he was born she placed him in swaddling clothes because it was cold, and she laid him in the manger. And she rejoiced in her motherhood, and commenced to hum to him, and to sing, and to chant lullabies to put him to sleep. And she gave him sustenance and comfort and spent much of the day and most of the night hugging him, and minding him, because he was her first-born. And the child looked back at her, and hummed, and sang, and made small gurgling childish noises. And she rejoiced even the more that he did not whinge and cry and cry his guts out as most children do. And Joseph rejoiced even more again, because Joseph was a man, and would not be expected to put up with the whinging and mewling and pewking and screaming of babies.

And some short time after that, when King Herod discovered that the so-called wise men from the east had fooled him, and had gone their own way without informing him of where the infant Jesus lay, he ordered and decreed that every male child under two years of age in the vicinity of Bethlehem be put to death. And the soldiers zapped through the town and ripped the children from their mothers' arms, or swept them from where they slept, or from where they played, and they hacked the heads off some of them, and chopped the legs off others, and extracted the nails from the fingers of yet more just for the fun of it, although the more humane of them drove their stakes through the children's hearts so as to get it over with quickly. They did this because they were soldiers of the emperor, and they were just obeying orders as soldiers of the emperor do, and just because there was a lot of big fat money going on the corpse of every child no matter what weight they were.

But by this time the baby Jesus and his mother and Joseph were safe and sound in Egypt. It hadn't been that difficult for them to escape since Jesus was always a good child, and had never cried nor bawled nor whinged.

But when the souls of the dead innocent babies left their bodies they sailed through the air to whatever place the souls of dead innocent babies go who have been murdered without mercy. But as they floated through the air one of them looked down on the infant Jesus, and he showed him his smashed skull, and his bloodied hands, and his extracted nails, and his little soul that had never been allowed to grow, and his pure undefiled body that had never had the oportunity to contemplate sin, and his spirit cried aloud to Jesus: 'This is all your fault!'

And the infant Jesus looked up at him from the straw in his manger and his eyes filled up with tears.

That was the very first time that Jesus wept.

The Judgement

ADAM HEARD THE MUSIC FIRST. I thought it was a ghettoblaster or some music store trying to flog their latest wares.

'Listen!' said Adam. 'I think he's out of tune.'

'Bloody sure he's not bloody Eddie Calvert,' said I, plucking a name out of the past. 'He wouldn't get a job with a bloody bad brass band.'

I had to admit I didn't feel that well since early morning. A shiver down my backbone and a quiver up my thighbone told me it wasn't going to be a lucky or a sunshiny day. The alarm clock failed to go off, Docila slept through, the children were late for school and a molar started acting up. The last time I felt as lousy as this the boss called me in and gave me a rise. This only went to prove I couldn't believe either my hunches or my bones.

Adam and myself were hoping to have a quiet lunch in the restaurant on the corner of the street but when he heard the music he gave me a dig in the ribs. There were others who noticed it also. Some grinned, some grimaced, all turned around looking for the music. I saw two guys starting to dance on the street but the rhythm screwed them up and they shagged off. I saw an old fellow scrunching the butt of a fag and hiding it under his coat despite the heat of the day.

Even though we were both starving we had to stop and listen. We thought the music was coming from the next street but when we went looking for it we always discovered it was still just one street away.

'Listen to that,' said a stranger next to me. 'You'd think we had enough electioneering by now. Lies and promises, promises and lies! What more are they good for?'

'Election, my arse,' said someone else, 'stay where you are and you'll see the greatest show on earth. Didn't you hear that the circus is coming to town?'

'It's all one big circus anyway,' said Adam, not entirely seriously. He was like that when he wanted to. We gave as good as we got when we needed to, but for some reason I felt a big grey lump growing quietly in my gut.

White fluffs of cloud dabbed the sky but they didn't cross the sun. I looked up to see two helicopters like fireflies racing above the city. I imagined by their frenzy that a bank had been robbed or terrorists had escaped from some prison and were now on the run. And then they vanished as if they had never fluttered the roofs of the houses.

'Come on,' said Adam, grabbing me by the elbow. 'Let's split. We can't spend the day staring at the sky. Fuck 'em all. Let's stuff our guts and let them all piss off.'

I was a bit reluctant to leave as long as there was a hullabaloo in the streets but hunger and convention won out. We sat down at the table where we had our lunch for nearly twenty years. We had a good view of the streets in case it was a *coup d'etat* or the boys were back in town.

'Just imagine the tanks rolling by,' said Adam, his mouth watering while he enjoyed and took pleasure from the thought. 'I'd give anything just for ten minutes of absolute power. Just ten minutes.'

'What would you do?' I asked, wondering about his grasp of the conditional mood.

'I have a little list,' he said, speaking in a conspiratorial hush in case anyone with big ears was listening. 'I have been compiling it for years. Every politician, every journalist, every sports commentator who has been a pain in the ass, they're all on the list.'

'It must be quite long so,' I said.

'As long as a wet day in County Mayo,' he said. 'I'd put them all into one big enormous tub. A huge transparent vat with a hole at the top just big enough for one person to go through simultaneously and at the same time.'

'You have been thinking about this for a while,' I said, as if I didn't know. It was always interesting to see if he had another turn of the screw or if anybody had been added to the list.

'Do you see that crane?' he asked, pointing his spoon in the direction of the tall construct waving about above the City Hall like a scorpion's tale about to strike. 'I'd hang my specially designed state-of-the-art tub off the top of that and do the hippy-hippy shakes up and around and topsy-turvy and head over heels so that just one of my chosen list would fall out, one at the time. That is the circus that I want. Just ten minutes.'

'Well, bully for you,' I said, thinking of my own list, 'but I'm afraid that whenever the coup comes neither you nor I will have much to do with it.'

'Speak for yourself,' he said, calling the waiter for something or other. 'I have military training just as well as you. You can't put that one over on me.'

'Five weeks in the FCA twenty years ago! I know of some petty dictators who still wouldn't have us. When the tanks roll up I'm going to stay sitting here smoking my cigar.'

If this was bullshit we were under the illusion it was good bullshit, and anyway if we couldn't pass muster we could at least pass the time. We all got whanged by life's vicissitudes but we still had our middle-aged dreams to keep us warm. Our ship would come in, or we would find the crock of gold at the end of the garden, or we would fall in love with a rich Jewish princess. Or at any rate we could keep talking as long as we had no other choice and there was no other thing to do nor any other place to go. O yes, we had our complaints, but it was better to curse the darkness than light a penny candle on a star.

'You better stuff yourself with that apple tart,' I said to Adam, having nothing better to say, 'you won't get anything as good as it until tomorrow. There's nothing worse than pangs of hunger in the smack-bang-middle of the high afternoon.'

He would do that anyway without any encouragement from me, but that didn't mean we were in any great hurry to pack up and go. To be on duty was not the same thing as to be in work. We still had time to gabble about the ex-President's mistress, the humour of the financial pages, ecological holidays in Greenland, the etymological derivation of the exclamation mark, the man who died of a broken fart which was great gas, and the pimp who thought everything was great crack. We paid a fortune for our lunch in order to help the economy as we did every day and we wearily wended our way back to the office.

Out on the street everyone was on the move. They all looked as if they were going in the same direction. There was a look in their eyes which had never been there before. You knew that even if you had never seen them until now. I tried to talk to one young fellow but he stared at me from out of eyes that welled up in tears.

Adam tried to chat up one woman but she laughed at him with a nervous highly-strung laugh.

I grabbed one old wrinkly by the elbow but he shook me off with a viciousness which I scarcely thought he could have.

Adam spoke to a child but no wisdom came forth from his mouth.

'Has the government fallen?' I shouted to the crowd.

'Fallen, my arse,' said one guy with a wart on his nose and vanished in the great wash.

'Has the stockmarket collapsed?' Adam pleaded, because he could be quite sensitive about these moneyed things when he had to be.

'Fuck the stock,' said another guy who looked to be about a thousand years old and never enjoyed a day in his life.

'Have the Brits attacked?' I shouted, falling back on the old enemy in time of necessity, but I only got an emphatic 'Not at this time' from a woman who was sucking her thumb.

'He's over there!' screamed a man between horrors and hosannas who had a rosary beads or a knuckle duster wrapped around his fist, and pointed us with his whole body to the corner of the road where we thought we had first heard the music.

'Who is it?' we both asked in unison and together, scarlet butterflies rising in our stomachs.

'This is the day I have been waiting for since the beginning of time,' the man said, and then grabbed us by the dirty scruff of our necks and shoved us forward to where the crowd was gawping up at the building.

'This is it now,' said your man, as happy as a kid going in to see Santa Claus, 'you're all fucked, you shower of fucking fuckers. Thanks be to God!'

'Who is he?' I asked, even plaintively, about the guy standing on the corner of the upper window who looked as if he was about to jump. 'Why doesn't somebody get the ambulance or the Gardaí? If he falls he'll make an awful mess.'

'Shut your face, you fool,' said your man again, a smile like a flea's arse flitting across his face. 'There's no chance of him falling. Don't you see his wings?'

He was, unfortunately, right. I had been paying attention to the trumpet in his right hand and to his unusual get-up and I hadn't noticed the two golden wings sticking out behind his back.

'Jaysus, I know who it is,' said Adam, nearly licking my ear, 'It's fucking Goldie Horn.'

I suppressed a chuckle as nobody else was chuckling, and anyway, this was real serious public shit rather than simple private angst.

'Or maybe it's Icarus,' I retorted. 'He's probably forgotten that we have airplanes for the last hundred years.'

'Judas Icarius,' said Adam, 'give him enough rope to hang himself.'

'It is written also,' said your man 'that thou shalt not go free because this is the day of accounting.'

'We had those accountants in last week,' said Adam, 'and they were some accuntants.'

Just then Willie Wings on the window let a great blast from his trumpet and everybody jumped back in horror. He laid down his trumpet and did produce a big red book from within his breast and commenced to read.

'Districts seven and eight,' he proclaimed, in a voice that had a certain eastern accent to it, 'that is to say, Cabra, Phibsboro, Arbour Hill, Stoneybatter, Inchicore, The Coom, The South Circular Road and adjacent areas, Section A; Districts three and nine, Clontarf, Ballybough, Clonliffe, Drumcondra, Whitehall, Santry and Griffith Avenue, Section B; Districts five and thirteen, Coolock, Artane, Raheny, Bayside, Barrytown, Sutton, Donnamede and Baldoyle, Section C; Districts one and six, Ranelagh, Rathmines, Rathgar, Terenure and Harold's Cross, Section D; District four, Donnybrook, Ballsbridge, Sandymount, Sandycove and Ringsend, Section E; Districts ten and eleven, Ballyfermot and Blanchardstown, Section F; District eighteen, Cabanteely, Foxrock, Cornelscourt ... '

People began moving away as their districts were called out, some obviously despondent, others proud and haughty, but nobody was saying very much. Whatever sounds there were came from the buzz of the announcements and the shuffle of feet beginning to move into the distance.

'Where are you?'

'Section E I think. I hear we'll get our entry cards at the gates.'

'What about the wife and kids?'

'It's everyone for himself now. That's the rule. Anyway they will have heard by now.'

'I don't know if I'm suitably dressed. My mother always told me to have clean underwear on me in case of an accident, or unforeseen circumstances. Maybe this is what she was warning me about.'

I turned around when I heard the newsboy shouting about the evening papers. The first edition was out earlier than usual because of the news.

'*Herald* or *Press*,' he roared, his voice reaching new heights of excitement. 'End of the world news! End of the world this afternoon! Official statement from heaven! Last judgement in the Phoenix Park!'

I shoved him the price of the paper and Adam looked in over my shoulder. According to their religious correspondent angels were landing in different locations all over the country since mid-day proclaiming the news. Judgement had already been given in most other European countries. The heavenly host was moving with the sun and wouldn't reach America until early in the morning Irish time. I suppose there was no such thing anymore as Irish time but it was difficult to get rid of the old metaphors. There was no hard data as yet available from the rest of the European Union because all the fax lines were clogged up and the Internet was acting funny. There was a small diagram at the bottom of the second page which purported to show unconfirmed figures for the number of saved and the number of damned in each country so far. It gave us some satisfaction to see that good Catholic countries like Spain and Portugal and even Italy had the highest saved rate. But Adam said that they also were the biggest producers of red wine, and that was the real reason. Against that there was a very high damnation rate in awful Protestant countries like Germany, Denmark and Finland, but England was the worst of all.

'Eighty-four per cent!' said Adam, in wonder and not a little satisfaction. 'That won't leave much room for us, thanks be to Jaysus.'

'Any mention of Purgatory?' I mentioned, scanning the page up and down, 'or the likes of Limbo?'

There wasn't, but there was more than enough speculation about who amongst the great and mighty and the eminent greasies of the country would go up and who would go down. The journalists were very kind to themselves but more than nasty to politicians whom they didn't like. They weren't too sure about the Cardinal as he had criticised the press the week before, but they did admit that if the Pope was saved that he had a very good chance also. I supposed this was an attempt to be fair now that the end was nigh. There was a full page of the detailed arrangements—the various routes to the Park, parking lots, the sites of the different pens into which people were to go, the tents of the Red Cross, fish and chip stalls, beer tables, bookies stands, photographers, toilets.

'They all seem to be walking anyway,' I said, as we had failed to hail a taxi, 'Let's go.'

We hit the road and joined the throng making its way to the Phoenix Park. Most of the people were quiet and reflective although there was the occasional murmer of prayer and the jangle of a rosary bead. Dublin Bus was providing a special cheap knock-down one-way fare but most people seemed to want to walk. I suppose it gave them a chance to stop and think every so often and to examine the state of their souls. Others were going back over the course of their lives trying to put it all together. The humour improved as we went on, however. We heard an occasional nervous laugh as if people were practicing confessions on one another.

'Do you remember?' Adam asked me reflectively, 'Do you remember you asked me once what would I do if I knew the end of the world was coming? Remember that?'

'I was talking about the Third World War then,' I said. We were passing by Phibsboro at this time and the road was getting congested at the major junction. 'We all thought it would happen that way. But I suppose since the Russians and Americans decided against frying us all God decided he'd have his pound of flesh anyway.'

'It's just as the poet said: "This is the way the world will end, this is the way the world will end, this is the way the world will end, not with a bang but with a wimpey."'

'And you said you'd go mad around the streets rubbing and robbing and plundering and whoring and fucking and blinding and doing all those things that only crawl under the skin of civilisation. And I said I'd blow my head off with a gun. Funny that we don't want to do any of those things now.'

'Life must go on,' he said wearily, 'that's the way it is—so it goes.'

'Last few ices, last few ices,' a vendor shouted, 'anyone now for the last few ice-creams.' He pushed his way through the crowd with skilled and sharp elbows.

There was a small bunch of angels standing guard outside Glasnevin Cemetery as we were going by. They had their golden swords drawn and had their backs to us. We thought this was a bit unusual until we saw them holding back the crowd inside. A motley collection of emaciated corpses, rotting bodies, skeletons, stiffs, cadavers and carcasses jostled at the gates trying to get out. It must have been that they were looking for a second chance. I have to say that they were not suitably attired to join the likes us on our way to the general judgement.

'Do you see de Valera?' shouted one woman, pointing out a lanky tall skeleton peering longingly through the bars of the gates.

'He hasn't changed much, anyway' said another.

'Except that he's a bit straighter now than he ever was,' said a third.

'So much for the treaty,' somebody mumbled.

'Who called him a traitor?'

There might have been a row only somebody joked that he could hardly be called the devil incarnate now, which drew the reply that he was at least the devil of Eire.

There were others who swore that they saw Roger Casement who would certainly know his way to the Phoenix Park; and yet others who said that it had to be Daniel O'Connell arguing with the angels with big rhetorical flourishes in the hope that he might be let out. Maybe he thought he had one more big speech in him before a captive audience.

We didn't have time to follow the discussion as we were

swept along in the tide of people away from the tide of history. It might have been interesting to have them along. They could have told us all that stuff the biographers never dug up. Ah well.

'Isn't it enough for anyone of us to be living in the present for none of us can be living forever and we must be satisfied,' said Adam, taking the words out of my mind. But he said many other things also which are not the matter of this story but which might be worth telling by somebody else some other time.

When we reached the Gates of the Phoenix Park the crowds were as thick as flies on a summer eve. They were coming from every direction, some on their own, some with their families, some with their second families, some others uncertainly with their present partners of similar gender or bent. Life was still ours but the future which beckoned was short. Guardian angels were posted every few yards giving directions and orders as required. We were all given identification cards on the other side of the Zoological Gardens. It would certainly be tragic if anyone was sent to Hell as a result of mistaken identity.

The great blue sky was awash with music as we approached the centre of the park. Those cherubim and seraphim must have been practising for eons and eons just for this one day. I couldn't quite see them yet but I could hear the brass and the boom and the hosannas and halleluias. I was lucky to be still with Adam although I must admit that Docila and the children did fleetingly cross my mind. If I didn't see them this side of the judgement it was unlikely I would see them on the other.

We had red cards and we followed all the directions

until we got to our pen. We were made sit on long wooden benches and told to wait until we were called. The odd vendor had sneaked in and was attempting to sell Coke or orange juice because it was a hot day. The angels didn't seem to bother too much about them. I think they were more worried about the ones who were trying to duck back in the queue and were giving bribes to people with holier faces. They were also trying to ensure that we kept our eyes glued on the giant movie screens that were posted around us showing different pictures. I was hoping to get a glimpse of the Judge and the throne and what was happening in the centre of the action but that didn't seem to be coming up yet. To tell you the truth they were quite interesting. We had a choice of about seven different screens but we could only concentrate on one at a time.

The one I was looking at was a kind of horror movie. For a moment I thought it was a video of what was going on in another part of the park. There were angels in it, I remember. Seven of them if I recall correctly. They had trumpets and were preparing to blow them. When the sound of the first trumpet was heard I did see a beast coming up out of the sea, having seven heads and ten horns, and upon its head ten diadems and curses spewing out of the mouths of the seven heads. And then another one blew his trumpet and I saw as it were a sea of glass mingled with fire and the fire was licking the rims of the mountains and the people were climbing up the mountains to escape from the fire. And when the third angel blew his trumpet the mountain rose up and crashed down into the sea and the sea became blood and swallowed up all the boats and the fish. This was like unto Krakatoa east of Java, only better! Then a star fell from heaven to earth and opened up a bottomless pit, and the pit belched up smoke that threw up poisonous scorpions and hydra-headed monsters and cookie zombies with papier maché make-up that wouldn't convince anyone. Grand if you like that kind of stuff but I felt it had all been done before. The producer of this movie wasn't very subtle, and anyway I don't think it scared anybody.

I suppose the idea was that it would pass the time and divert our attention from the moving queues going past us to the place of judgement. We tried to stand up every so often in order to stretch our limbs but we were really trying to get a glimpse of the bench.

'Did you see him yet?' Adam asked me, after I did a little hop and a jump.

'I don't think so,' I said, 'he appears to be entirely surrounded by the Deitorium Guards. I think he's tall, slender, blonde, bearded and blue-eyed.'

'He has no beard,' a wise-looking guy next to me said, speaking as if he really knew something that the rest of us didn't. 'He as bald as a baby's bum, as well-dressed and groomed as any chief executive of a big company.'

'I heard that,' said a red-headed man courteously, 'and I beg to oppose. I saw him a few moments ago and he was big, fat and hairy. Quite like the Pope actually, apart from his fine head of hair.'

'Ye're all wrong ye ignorant slobs!' A woman was standing on a seat wringing her hands and mouthing at us in a brassy voice. 'She's a woman I'm telling ye! A big strong power-dressed woman with glasses! I saw her.'

'Yes, and I suppose she is black too, and wears a 'Save

the Whales' button, and is eating a macrobiotic sandwich,' I said, but I don't think anyone heard me. They were too busy holding forth about what God looked like but I think in the end we had to agree that nobody had really seen him. A few people might have got clocked if it wasn't for the angelic police keeping a close eye on us. Adam said he was a bit pissed off with all this theology stuff although he did admit he was getting excited at the prospect of meeting Him. If it was only that He was the biggest cheese of all in the history of the world and that he wanted to satisfy his own curiosity.

When we saw the people in the pen next to us getting up and being organised into queues we knew our time was not long off. They were moving along so briskly that it dawned on me there could have been more than one judge, or else he had a few assistants like Santa Claus at Christmas. Or else again that you didn't get much chance to plead your case. Maybe it was all written down in the Big Book of Judgement and your fate was sealed ever before you got to the bench.

A strange quietness came upon us and the banter died away as we were told to stand up and be ready. This was the day and the hour of which we didn't know. I gritted my teeth and a weird tingle went down my spine when we were ordered into our queue for the long walk along the beaten track of the green, green grass to where our home would be decided. Now was the time for examining our conscience for the last time and weighing up the good with the bad. I remembered all my vices with some affection—pride, covetousness, lust, gluttony, anger, envy and sloth—but I couldn't say I was particularly good at any one of them. I also had many virtues, but it would be a vice to enumerate them. If there was sometimes evil in my heart there was also charity. I had no machine with which to weigh them against one another, however. How could you measure cigarettes and whiskey and wild, wild women against doing your duty and saying your prayers and voting for the government? Anyway, I'd soon know the answer. The same questions must have been bugging Adam because he had got very quiet. Or maybe he had just remembered some big bad sin that had escaped him until now.

The queue stretched out as far as my eyes could see, yea, nearly unto the ends of the park. There seemed to be still millions packed into the pens on each side of us, and needless to say they weren't green with envy. We got prodded with batons every so often to keep us moving, and I even saw one guy getting thumped by an angel for dawdling. After a while the judgement area began to become clearer but we were still too far away to guess what was happening. I was amazed how quickly we were moving, almost like a Sunday afternoon stroll.

'Make way! Make way!' a guard shouted at us and pushed us to one side rather roughly. A huge lorry was making its way along the track and was being driven by two angels. Its siren went through our ears like glass cutting through bone. It swept past us in a swirl of dust and we were allowed crawl back into the centre of the passageway.

'What was that all about?' I heard one guy ask impatiently.

'Did you not see what was on the back of the lorry?'

'Skins,' said somebody or other, 'I saw another few lorries just like that when I was coming in a few hours ago. One of the angels told me they were sheep and goat skins. We are all given one or the other of them after sentence has been passed—depending on where we are going.'

'It was mostly goatskins so on that last load.' This much was spoken by a large lugubrious mountain of a man for whom any kind of a fitting would have been a professional challenge for the heavenly tailors. 'They must be in great demand.' This much spoken resignedly.

I should have been surprised by the petty conversation going on all around me but I wasn't. Life was too important to be left to the philosophers. I overheard one woman asking her friend if she thought God would be as goodlooking or as sexy as Brad Pitt, but then she suddenly remembered she had forgotten to hang out the wash. What looked to me like a fancy rugger-bugger was discussing his golf handicap with another guy who was only interested in car upholstery. A priest ahead of us spent his time looking into a pocket mirror and combing his hair. There were, of course, others whose faces were ashen and drawn as if they knew that the wages of sin were about to be paid. On the other hand there wasn't much point in throwing yourself on the ground with wailing and gnashing of teeth.

'Would you mind if I went first, I mean go ahead of you?' Adam asked me as we began to approach the judgement throne.

'Would I mind?' I said incredulously. 'Of course you can. Those few seconds might make all the difference between everlasting torment and an eternity of celestial bliss. Go ahead!'

By this time we could get a good look at the judgement throne and at God himself. There was a huge angel standing on his right-hand side. He was wearing formal evening clothes with a green carnation in the lapel. A big leather-bound volume was open before him. There were a few other angels lolling about the throne also but they were obviously getting bored with everything. Two lines stretched out on both sides behind the throne but it was clear that the one to the left with the people wearing the goatskins was much longer than the other. The angel giving out the sheepskins was more or less redundant.

Our ears were pricked up the closer we got to the interrogation. It was difficult to follow every word at first but I soon began to get the gist of it. It appeared that God would say something, and then the angel would ask a question and the person would be whisked away after that. I found myself hiding behind Adam, but I knew that I couldn't get away with that for long.

'I see you're not wearing a tie,' I heard the angel say to a teenager just a little bit ahead of us, 'Go to hell!'

'In the hoond of the cakes, purples or aflamed with cloaks,' I heard God say to the next guy, 'Foreplicate that forum, o Muckle.'

'God says that you're all right,' the angel said stretching out a hand towards the heap of sheepskins, 'I'm told you went to the right school.'

'Oily zounds!' God said, looking at the nice young woman who was next, 'bydeboils alanna buddy hast a vein twinpeekaboozies and whale clonking doanlast didgiridoo. Dattbee a through ghostspill, you bedda boleweevil me!'

'Bye-bye, farewell, aufwiedersehen, goodnight,' said

Muckle the angel to her, 'he didn't like your clothes. Next!'

The next up was an elderly man who looked scholarly and pious. He took off his hat and curtsied politely.

'Who the fofo costuree me?' said God, 'A burden in the bosh wotnot joice addlerup pound for pound. Amon aye right? 'Botchito ergo sum samizdat I pray tallways.'

'Put on your goatskin,' said Muckle, 'you ain't got no ticket for heaven. You should have bought it when you had the chance. It's too late now.'

'Whoroo the lustie dabbie plunking the plushty?' God asked the next young girl, who had obviously put on her very best dress for the occasion. 'Or oroo the chickybiddy whang woofs the woost waddie joke buzzer? Whorov the squidge and squish ovdat hah!'

'He has just asked you if you know the third law of thermodynamics,' said Muckle interpreting for her, 'but as it is perfectly plain that you haven't the least clue you better fuck off down to hell.'

I was looking very carefully at the priest because if anyone had a passport he surely did. He stood up directly and made a brief humble bow before turning his head ever so slightly towards the judgement throne. God looked kindly down on him and smiled widely from ear to ear showing a perfectly formed row of golden teeth.

'I om the Ram of Gob,' he said, 'and thee pissed a balls prophet. The dimple tooth you buggerup and you bekim alloy for alloy. As furry high cough earned ukan shakov. Jew dearme?

'But I spread your word, I preached the gospel,' the priest protested, as he didn't really need a translation, I kept all the commandments, I followed the truth ... '

'The truth?' Muckle snorted, turning towards God with a query on his brow, 'what is this truth thing of which he speaks?'

'Oh snot daffleclut to hobble that,' said God, 'the tooth is sumpty this, and sumpty that and sumpty sumpty else.'

'He says that you were consistent,' smiled Muckle handing him a goatskin, 'and that the truth is sometimes this, and sometimes that and sometimes the other. But you were too tied down to see that. Off you go!'

The next guy didn't have any identity card, the woman who came after him didn't have enough money, and the man after her again didn't have the right measurements. They were all damned. A quiet woman just ahead of us was given the benefit of the doubt because she had nice curly hair and was a distant relation of a nun. She skipped away happily and Adam took three steps up to his judgement.

'Come closer,' grunted Muckle, as Adam seemed a little reluctant and not too surprisingly. I was afraid I'd soil my pants when I came next, or else no words would come out of my tongue. My mouth was dry and my lips were cracked and my knees were weak. Adam didn't appear to me to be so frightened but he never was one to let the big occasion get him down. I could see everything perfectly clearly now. The big stream of the damned going off to the left and vanishing down a hole in the ground; the small trickle going off to the right and ascending a shining escalator which appeared to vanish in the blue of the sky. I could also see the face of God and it was clear that he was enjoying every minute of this. There was a permanent smile glued to his face as of somebody wielding power that had never been wielded before. He would take off his glasses every so often but it didn't change the serenity of the smile. If it wasn't this particular day and this particular afternoon that would never come again even the most gloomy person would have to enjoy the balmy sun and the easy warmth.

'Fot is the fie or the fairfore ovoo?' God asked gently, 'or waywho war wore rootings, whore poor ants?'

'He is asking you what you have ever done for the environment?' said Muckle, a bit grudgingly.

'I have to admit that I have done nothing at all,' said Adam in a kind of a pally way. I thought this was quite inappropriate. 'I mean really nothing. And, come to think of it, I have done nothing either for my neighbours. Or for the state, or for the church, or for the poor, or for the third world. In fact, every single thing I have ever done has been for myself alone. Just me. That's me in a nutshell.'

'Well that's it so,' said Muckle. 'Take yourself off to hell. We have no time here for liars. I know that you once gave a penny to charity when you were a little boy and you could have spent it on sweets. You lied, you bastard! You're not as bad as you make yourself out to be. So fuck off out of my sight.' He handed him a mangy-looking goatskin on which there was a large brown stain.

Adam took it from him quietly and was just turning away when I heard the bang. I spun round and saw two holes in God's chest with his life's grace pouring out of them where he had been plugged. I saw the gun in Adam's hand and Muckle drawing the sword from his scabbard. I saw another hole blown in Muckle's skull as he flopped to the ground. I saw the other guards coming with their swords at the ready but they were no match for an automatic pistol. I heard the death-rattle in God's throat as if he was trying to say something to the world as he was leaving it. I wasn't really able to understand them as he never was a very clear speaker. I thought it was something like 'Dally the llhama, it is spaghettini' but I couldn't be sure.

'Now that God is dead,' Adam said to the world the following day, 'we may as well begin all over again. And this time there will be logic and order and justice and peace.'

We gave God a good funeral and made sure there was a respectable crowd there. I couldn't attend myself as I was too busy making sense of our new world and was beginning to enjoy the power.

Knackers

WHEN MARY AND JOSEPH REACHED Bethlehem they were totally whacked out. Even the old donkey had had enough. They would have slept anywhere only Mary felt pains coming on and felt she needed some bed, any bed, to lie on. The first inn they tried was full of gamblers and dice-throwers and three-card trick merchants honing their skills in preparation for the influx of yokels and culchies from the surrounding countryside. Joseph steered them away. Then they came to an inn that was full of soldiers and census counters and functionaries of the emperor with their lackeys and hangers-on. The street outside was awash with people carousing, and others singing, and some getting sick in the gutters. One drunken soldier tried to talk to the donkey but when he didn't get any intelligible reply decided he had enough and lay down to dream.

Joseph thought it better to escape to the edge of the town where things were quieter and where the crowds were much thinner. He saw a small family inn just beside an olive tree with a single light outside the door. It looked clean and well-kept and safe. There were no drunks hanging around outside and no raucous singing coming from the inside. The innkeeper was a jolly chubby man who looked as if he enjoyed his lamb chops and his pitcher of wine.

'Hello,' he greeted Joseph, 'how can I help you?' In another day and age he might have said 'Have a nice day,' but he didn't.

'I need a room for the night, maybe two,' Joseph said, and explained his plight and his circumstances.

The innkeeper listened to him carefully, and then said smiling from ear to ear and from tooth to tooth, but not from eye to eye: 'Sorry, full up. Too bad. Not tonight.'

But when he saw the despair in Joseph's eye he relented a little and said, 'Look there's a bit of a barn out the back. You can kip in there for the night if you like. Just don't disturb the animals.'

And when Joseph and Mary and the donkey had gone away the innkeeper's daughter came down the stairs in a rage.

'Daddy,' she said, 'what did you do that for? You know the inn is half empty. There's bags of room. Nobody comes out here to this buttend of town. Why did you send them away?'

'Did you not hear them?' the innkeeper replied. 'Did you not hear his accent? They're not from the right address. The proprietor reserves the right to refuse admission. They could be knackers for all I know. And anyway, didn't you see the woman? She was pregnant!'

Greater Love Than This

WHEN THEY TOLD PAT'S WIFE THAT he was dead she cried until she could cry no more. She dressed herself in black clothes and she tore her hair from its roots. She cried again even though her eyes were dry and could give no more water.

Those dry white tears fell on her scoured cheeks. She spoke dark and heartbroken words to all who came near her. She could not open her ears to words of charity or consolation.

They laid her husband's body out in the bed and she spoke sweet and sorrowful words to him between bouts of wailing and screaming. She did not sleep that first night, nor the second.

Every waking minute they had spent together rushed through her mind, all the joy and the happiness and the love they had shared ended in this cold shroud.

She threw herself on his body while he lay on the bed. She kissed him passionately on his cold, cold lips while he lay in his coffin. She would not let them put the lid on it until they had no choice, and even then they couldn't secure it.

She was dragged screaming into the funeral car on the

day of the burial. She nearly died of grief every inch of the way to the graveyard. Greater love than this no woman ever had for a man, nor any wife for a husband.

When they lowered the coffin into the grave she let out a piercing cry which reached up to heaven and tore down deep into the earth.

And while she did not succeed in throwing herself into that black hole after her husband's coffin she ensured that it was filled with beautiful flowers rather than with clay. Thousands and thousands and thousands of flowers and wreaths and bouquets of every colour and smell were piled into that grave wherein her husband was laid.

But when Pat woke up in his coffin some short time later he realised he wasn't in his own bed. He raised the lid of the coffin just a fraction and his nose was filled with the sweet and fragrant smell of flowers. But he could not lift it any further because of the heavy weight of love pressing him down.

The Gifts of the Magi

BUT WHILE JESUS AND MARY AND Joseph were still in Bethlehem they were visited by three travellers out of the east who gave them three Christmas presents. Joseph certainly knew what the gold was as he had seen it glitter in the temple, and on the rings of the high priests as they flashed them against the sun, and on the necklaces of the wives of the roman bosses as they showed who was who. He wasn't sure what to do with the frankincense but it sure smelt nice, and he thought the myrrh resin might be some use in sticking furniture together.

But when the angel came to him in his dream and told him to shift himself fast and flee into Egypt with his family because Herod and his crew were after him, he knew he had to move as speedily as possible.

'Take nothing with you,' the angel had warned him, 'only the barest necessities.'

They didn't have much with them anyhow but he dumped most of the swaddling clothes, hiding it in the straw in case they might leave a clue for the soldiers. 'You still have too much,' the angel whispered in his ear, as they left the stable, 'You'll never get to Egypt in time.'

He threw his hammer and chisel behind him on the

road as he wasn't likely to need them in the place he was going. 'You still have too much,' the angel whispered, 'you'll never make it.'

He thought of chucking his sandals but he knew he would need them in the heat of the desert. There was no point in taking the sacking from the donkey's back as Mary needed whatever protection she could. He bit his lip hard and breathed deeply and knocked on the innkeeper's door. The innkeeper was half asleep it being the middle of the night and he being in the middle of a very pleasant dream. He nearly hit Joseph when he opened the door.

'This is for you,' Joseph said, handing him a parcel. 'It's for your kindness to us in loaning us the stable when everyone else turned us away. I have no other way of paying you. I hope this is enough.'

The innkeeper grabbed the parcel and went back to sleep. 'Here,' he said to his daughter the following morning, 'you can have the smelling oils. I'll hang on to the metal. I often got tin from knackers, but this is the first time I got gold.'

The Poet Who Died And Went To Hell

A POET DIED.

This in itself is a rare and unusual occurance because poets are normally thought to be immortal. It was even suggested that this poet committed suicide because he wrote a bad poem.

He was raised up to the gates of heaven so that he might be judged and that his bad poem could be weighed against the other good works of his life.

'I'm very sorry,' Peter of the Gates said, since he had read what the critics and reviewers had to say, 'you can't come in here. And anyway the joint is overflowing with poets. You have to go to the other place. They actually need some poets to keep the whole crew of theologians, theosophists and lawyers and liars amused.'

Even though the poet was undoubtedly disappointed he had some experience of being rejected.

He had never received a bursary from the arts council, nor given readings before the president, nor gone on reading junkets away and abroad.

'Look, just suppose,' he said to Peter, keeping his tears back because he knew he would need them in the other place, 'just suppose I did get in, could you tell me how would I spend the day, what do you do to pass the time within the pearly gates?'

'O, that's not a difficult question,' said Peter. 'You would spend your time listening to poetry being read. Paul and Paula and Theo and Phil and Seamus and Ciarán and Nuala and Derek and TS and RS and Ted and Alfred and William and silly Willy, they're all here.'

'Well, good for them,' he said, and off he went with his tail, or whatever, between his legs.

When he reached the sulpher gates the welcoming party was waiting for him dressed in police uniform.

'Look, before I come in,' he said, the poet said, 'would you mind telling me how I will spend the day, what do you do to pass the time within the sulpher gates?'

'O, that's not a difficult question to answer,' said a devil, devilishly. 'You will spend the day listening to poetry being read.'

'Well, isn't that just deadly,' said the poet. 'There is nothing I prefer more than to listen to poetry being read from the crack of dawn to the drawing down and dying of the light. What poetry will I listen to?'

'Your own, of course,' was the reply, 'for all eternity.'

The Postmodernist

HE LIVED IN THE MOST COSMOPOLITAN country in the world and ate in the most ritzy Chinese restaurants whenever he liked. It wasn't that he was averse to Indian food, but he usually wasn't hot on it as it didn't agree with his stomach, or with other parts of him somewhat lower down. He wore Gucci shoes quite simply because he had the money to buy them. He fancied Versacci-designed clothes although it is unlikely that Versacci fancied him anymore. He had paintings by Picasso and Constable and Ronaldi adorning his walls (but they weren't originals, of course). He recalled having been in love with a mountainous woman from Tibet, and yet another from Easter Island who was particularly upright and strong. He abandoned his native religion and spent a while as an atheist before converting to the Mormons because he liked their manners; he thought later that Buddhism had possibilities because it was modish among musicians and film-stars. He travelled through Patagonia because he had read the book, and he wished to walk on the Great Wall of China because he heard it could be recognised from the moon. He had books of poetry by Nikolai Liliev (the Bulgarian one), and by Vincenzo Monti even though he couldn't persuade anybody else of his brilliance; he admired Vladimir Solukhin's experiments in free verse, and was turned on by the force of Alfred Lichtenstein's work. As regards music he had catholic taste. His ears delighted in Moussa Poussy and Ronnie Fruge and The Cajun Kings, not to mention Papa Wemba and Kostatin Verimozov and Mahmoud Tabrizi Zadeh and Marta Sebestyen (in particular), although he did have to admit that he drew a line at the saccharine emenations of Daniel O'Donnell and others of his ilk. He could gobble potatoes from Cyprus or drive a Japanese car. He remembered some French from school, and had learned some tourist Spanish, and knew some German from those war films. He had a book of Latin because he was going to Latin America, and some Finnish for use in the Sauna, and very fluent English which had thousands of foreign words through it.

When he died, however, he was buried in a coffin of dark Irish oak, as was only proper.

Progress

THERE WAS A PERFECTLY HAPPY MAN who lived underneath a tree. He ate the fruit and the nuts that fell often and in abundance into his lap. He was never hungry.

He never had to stir a limb nor shake a leg nor wiggle an extremity except when he had to answer the call of nature.

One day a student came his way. He was studying business and entrepeneurship in the University of Limerick and walked with a swagger as if he was a Cork hurler.

'Look,' he said to the lazy dosser underneath the tree, 'look at the great and wonderful opportunity you are missing to make money and get on in the world. Instead of eating this fruit and chewing these nuts why don't you collect them all together and sell them to the shops, or at the market, or at the fair? Or even better than that, why don't you plant some of them in the ground so that other trees might grow, and more fruit would fall, and greater nuts will come, and you should make an even bigger and fatter profit?'

'And why would I want to do that?' said the lazy man under the tree out of a half-closed eye.

'So that you would make money, of course.'

'And why would I want to make money?'

Even though the student from the University of Limerick didn't really understand the question he tried to answer it as best he could because the education which he had received hadn't quite erased or banished the good manners which he naturally possessed.

'Well,' said the student, 'if you had enough money you could do anything at all you liked. Maybe, even, you wouldn't have to do any thing at all. You could be idle all day long. You could rest and take it easy.'

'And what do you think I am doing now?' asked the man who lived under the tree.

Revenge

FOR NO PARTICULAR REASON THE Emperor's Army attacked without warning.

In that first year they killed about a million people give or take some thousands who weren't that important.

The next year about another million died from hunger and starvation but this may not be an accurate account as most of the government officials were busy with estimates of wealth and of minerals.

The following year another million left the country as refugees in small boats and through tunnels and over barbed wire and across minefields.

The year after that the Emperor's soldiers raped a million women and boasted about it—but not to the international press.

The next year again a million children had their hungry swollen bellies pierced with sharp steel bayonets which soon shut them up.

Then one day a poor misguided simpleton killed one of the Emperor's soldiers. He was arrested.

'Why did you do that?' they asked him during interrogation. 'Did you not know that he was married? Did you not know that he had two children and that his wife was expecting a third? Did you not know that he was a lovely guy, very kind and considerate, loved animals, went to church, did charity work, had a great sense of humour, only lived for his family, wouldn't hurt a flea and only joined the Army because he was unemployed? What kind of a lowlife mindless bastard are you to kill an honest soldier of the Emperor?'

'Yes, I know I am a lowlife mindless bastard to so kill an honest soldier of the Emperor,' the man admitted while he protected his face with nailless fingers, 'But do you not think that the Emperor might have had just a teeny-weeny bit to do with it also?'

The Royal Fate

WHEN THE KING, THE QUEEN AND the princess were fleeing from justice they hid for the night in a tavern not far from the border. Their escape had been lucky and the cry of tortured subjects, widowed women and orphaned children rang in the sky. They probably did not hear them because of the cultured music which hummed in their ears.

They wore rags and tried to speak like humans. It was particularly difficult to flatten vowels as their mouths were swollen with generations of talk which never touched the ground. It was difficult to eat with soft hands that never cleaned a baby's bottom nor scoured a pot but nobody grew suspicious until the king found it hard to drink his wine. This was because of a snot which floated around on the top of his mug and which was not unusual in this place.

Ears were listening when they went upstairs to sleep. The king said nothing and the queen said nothing when they climbed into bed for fear of the ears that might be listening. A kind of sleep fell upon them as they were jacked out from their journey.

But the poor (metaphorically) princess could not sleep

at all at all despite her tiredness. Well, she did doze for a brief few minutes but all the king's horses and all the king's men couldn't get poor princess to sleepy again. She moaned and groaned and whinged and pouted and foamed and cried because she was a princess and this is what princessess are good at.

'What's wrong with you?' her mother asked, 'be quiet or we'll be caught,' she said into her ear in a whisper.

'I can't help it,' said the princess between whinges and moans and groans, 'there's a lump in the bed.'

Her mother, being a mother, ran her hand along the bed and above the mattress but she could find no lump with her smooth and bathed palm.

'But that doesn't mean it's not there,' said her daughter with tears and sighs and no footmen nor pages to sooth her.

Just then the crude democratic crew burst in through the door with dirty nails and rough hands and bad breath and flat vowels. One of them stuck his hand in under the mattress and took it out.

'Is this what you were looking for?' he asked, holding a tiny pea between pointed forefinger and crude thumb.

And that was how they knew they had the royal family.

And that is how they lost their heads from their necks as a result of one little tiny pea.

The Shepherds

THE SHEPHERDS WERE VERY SILENT AS they made their way back to the hill. They hoped their sheep would still be there and not devoured by mountain wolves who savaged their flocks when they went unguarded. As they returned they felt in their heart that the earth was fragrant and the sky was full of the jewels of the universe.

'So what was that all about?' asked one of them, who was later to leave the hillside and venture to Athens as a bad philosopher.

'It was a birth, it was the future,' said another, 'no future no livelihood, no livelihood no sheep, that's logic.'

'I don't give a fig for the future,' yet another said, giving birth to a phrase which would even baffle etymologists if they cared to go back that far, 'I want to know where he came from, who his people were. We can't be expected to leave our work and go for a canter down into the town to see some class of a baby just because a bunch of extra-terrestrial fairy types materialise out of thick air and tell us to hump off. And yet, he was quite a nice baby, I have to give him that much even though I haven't seen too many.'

'Just as well my wife wasn't here,' said a shepherd with a

thick lip, 'she'd have seen that he was like everyone on earth, she's like that, no subtlety, likes to please everyone, might have even said he looked like me, or even herself, you know the way it is.'

'But he did look like your wife,' said a small humpbacked shepherd with inverted knees, 'he did look like her, and also like the towncaller, and had some resemblance to the deacon, and the undertaker's daughter, and the teacher's mate, and the politician's nephew, and the minister's friend, and the cobbler's latest, and the tailor's dummy, and John O'Dreams, and Max Headroom, he looked like them all in general, and yet I'm not sure he looked like any of them in particular.'

'I'm sure he looked like himself,' said a careful one who was never wrong and never right and never had any friends.

'We'll have to answer for this,' said another, who had sneaked some straw from the manger, and was obviously trying to draw a conclusion, which was particularly difficult for him as he wasn't in the least bit artistic.

'I'll tell you,' said one guy who ever only made the most weighty of statements, 'I have no doubt but that he was like his mother. The spitting image.'

'Sure as hell,' said his sidekick who thought himself a bit of a halfwit, 'sure as hell he wasn't like his father,' and continued laughing into his dribble.

The sheep stood before them on the hill huddled against the cold. You would think they had never moved since their minders had gone into the town two nights before. For a moment they thought that one of their lost sheep had returned, but they couldn't be certain.

'I know who he was like,' said one of the company in a

voice of such certainty that it may have shook the faith of the mountain.

'Good for you,' they said, 'tell us more.'

'He had the face of a shepherd,' the man on the mountain said, 'a very good shepherd. That's what he had. The face of a good shepherd.'

Falling Out of Love

'SHE LEFT YOU THEN?'

'Yes, some other guy. You know how it is.'

'That's tough. That's real tough.'

'You said it. Don't I know.'

'But then it's an old story. Happens all the time. To me. To you. To everybody. So it goes.'

'As you say, it's an old story. But it's a new pain every time.'

The Singer and the Song

THE CHIEF WIZARD OF THE ONE and only true faith was much loved and highly regarded. He travelled the world in his golden plane and kissed the ground in humility and thanksgiving when he landed safely. He shook hands with the great and mighty with their baby-seal-lined gloves and waved at the poor and lonely who gawped on the balconies.

High or mighty, poor or lowly, they all loved his words of wisdom. Money flowed in—even when he didn't ask for it—after a particularly good television appearance, Chequebooks and purses and wallets and bank accounts were opened as quickly as any poor person might say 'God help me' or 'Why doesn't God help me?' Rich and good people loved him, and kings and emperors adored him, and presidents of rich countries whose people were fat and forgetful slobbered over his sweet and beautiful words.

'Love the poor,' he would say with a kind of sincerity that could not be denied, 'but remember the poor you will have with you always.'

'Love justice and righteousness,' he would say solemnly through his loudspeaker to the crowd, 'but remember to render unto Caesar the things that are Caeser's and anything else after that isn't God's.'

'Don't love worldly things,' he might say, 'but remember that the labourer is worthy of his hire and never refuse what is rightly yours and earned by the sweat of your brow or any other kind of sweat.'

These were the kind of words that showed that God was in his Heaven and all was well with the world—at least in the northern hemisphere or where geographers called 'the first world'.

One day, however, he changed his tune. He did this suddenly without any warning. There was no easy explanation for this and even psychobiographers were baffled. It might have been sunstroke the more literal tried to explain, or a kick from a horse, or a nightmare or even just one of those things. It was as if the conditional clause was excised from his brain by a form of grammatical circumcision.

'Sell all you have and give it to the poor,' he would say without pause or hesitation.

'Justice and whatever is right even if the sky falls,' he would say and stop with a full stop as big as a library.

'Don't kill. Don't steal. Don't fornicate. Don't curse.' He would say this as if it was the most natural thing in the world and if he had been saying it for years.

'Pay no heed for tomorrow. Do not save or store. Look at the swallows. They neither reap nor sow and yet God minds them. Live for today. Love everybody even if they fuck you up.' You know the kind of stuff.

So it wasn't any surprise when they started to abandon him.

Some threatened the law. Others hanging or thumb screws. Others said it was blasphemy. Others said he should be stoned if he wasn't already.

He had to escape in the middle of the night and retreat to the desert where truth was either wet or dry.

'Now, I know,' he said while he spoke to the stones in his cave, 'I always thought that they loved me. But it appears that they only loved the nice things that I said.'

Story in One Hundred Words

IT BEGAN TO BE NOTICED that the road signs and directions around the city were being stolen.

This was strange because it could hardly be imagined that there was a market for such stuff.

After that the names of streets went missing.

This confused the police and the authorities because they couldn't see any pattern or logic to it.

One day the northside, next day the centre, third day nothing.

Just by accident they caught the culprit.

Some class of an artist, you'd say, by his beard.

When asked to explain, he simply said: 'I was trying to help education.'

The Stain

THE GREY MIST WOULD HAVE ENTERED my soul if I had not reached the town before dark. The slip and slap of wipers could only keep away the damp but not the unrelieved darkness which reigned beyond the lights of the car. The town was grey apart from a few dim lamp-posts which reluctantly shone on the main street. It took an act of faith to believe that there were other streets crawling off to each side but there must have been as this was a town that was marked on the map.

'Two bottles a day,' my friend would say about towns like this. 'Two bottles a day, Scotch or Irish, that's what it would take to survive in this town.'

Whatever about two bottles I felt I needed at least one hot whiskey after a decent meal before I went to bed. There wasn't likely to be any night clubs in a place like this and whatever wild oats I had were long since sown in bigger towns around the country.

I checked into the only hotel at the bottom of the main street and the girl at the desk didn't even ask if I needed commercial rates. I must have looked it all over from the boredom in my eyes to the drag at the bottom of my feet.

She tried to smile but failed. She must have failed just about everything else too or she wouldn't be working in a hotel like this in a town like this on a night like this.

Although the menu looked promising I soon learnt that it always did.

'I'm afraid we don't have the salmon tonight, sir,' the same girl said, poised with her much-chewed pencil.

'I'll try the steak, then,' I ventured.

'It's very tough. The cook doesn't recommend it.'

I was going to say that all my teeth were false so it didn't matter but I was too hungry.

'What about the chicken?'

'We've run out of that, sir.'

'No chance of the venison, dear?'

'That's not on the menu, I'm afraid.'

'Then, what is on the menu?'

'Most people have the mixed grill, sir.'

So did I. It was alright except the egg kept sliding away and hiding behind the bacon while the black pudding acted as blotting paper for the yolk. As a result I got to the bar more quickly than I supposed but she was there before me again.

'Could I have the menu, please,' I said as I tried to find a level spot for the barstool on the floor.

'But you've already eaten,' she said.

'I mean the bar menu,' I said, 'just to see what I can drink.'

She still looked puzzled so I didn't push it but just ordered my hot whiskey and settled down to read the paper. Some journalist was defending some awful referee and attacking the GAA for appointing him. His colleague was explaining why they all got the result of last Sunday's match wrong and pontificating about what would happen next week. I often thought if sports journalists were paid by the accuracy of their predictions there would be a lot of them out of a job.

'A bad night.'

He was anything between thirty and sixty, balding on top and reddening in the face and he was sitting next to me. All the worries of the universe were written across his brow and I knew I was going to hear about them all. I winced and looked away but I had to say something.

'A bad night,' but I didn't add 'surely.'

'Been like this for weeks now.'

'For years,' I said.

'They say it's not going to get any better either,' he said, lifting his half-pint, turning it around and setting it down again. A half-pint man meant he wasn't going to get either stroppy or sloppy.

'I'd say they're right too,' I said.

'It's the sheep on the hills' he said, 'when they stay close to the meadow it's not a good sign.'

'You never spoke a fairer word,' I said.

'And things bad enough as they are.'

'We all have our troubles.'

'Too true, too true.'

At this stage in such a conversation, if that's what it was, you can either get up and leave, keep on blathering, tell him to get stuffed, make up some tall yarn, talk about some boring football match, swap dirty jokes, bitch about the state of the country or just or go for it. As the television in the corner appeared to be broken I went.

'What's yours, then?' I asked, looking him straight in the yellows of his eyes.

'What's my what?' he said, shocked that anyone wouldn't go round the kitchen and home by the dresser.

'What's your trouble? What's bugging you? What do you want to get off your chest? The bee in your bonnet, the fly in your ointment, the chip on your shoulder, the spider in your net, the ants in your pants, the howzyerfather in the whatzyergranny?'

He backed off a bit. 'Ah, you wouldn't be interested. You're educated.'

'Try me,' I said, 'nobody's education is ever finished.' He'd never know how true that was. I once thought that Hitler's first name was 'Heil' in a pub quiz.

'It's the youngfella,' he said, looking away again as if he was ashamed. 'Came home the other day from school. Got the sheer hite beaten out of him. Won't go back now. Says some brother did it. Has a funny name. Some kind of a dog. Brother Baywolf, I think.'

I laughed to myself and then I stopped. It was funny ha-ha that someone could so easily confuse a nickname with a real one, but it was funny peculiar that there could be two Brother Baywolfs in all the southern province.

'This Brother—whatzizname—Baywolf,' I asked, 'what does he look like?'

'Not sure myself,' he said, 'but Simon—that's the lad — says he's a nasty little runt. Nose like a geometry problem, he says. Teeth like a wall in Beirut. Big jam-jar glasses. A tuft of hair like the last of the Ma Higginses. Two dimples like a bicycle rack. Shoulders like King Kong.'

That was him. It couldn't be anyone else. God could

only make one aberration at the same time with the same name for all his power.

'You're a liar, Mac,' he had shouted at me after the duster missed. 'You're a filthy, nasty, lowdown, sneaky liar.'

'I'm not Bro, honest.'

'The word is honestly, Mac, It's an adverb Mac, and you wouldn't know what it meant if it grabbed you by the trousers. Isn't that right?'

'Yes, Bro.'

'No, Mac, it can't be right. If you say one thing it must be the other because you are constitutionally incapable of telling the truth. But I'll tell you this much, Mac. I'm going to get you to tell the truth today if it's the last thing I do. Because I have a duty to get you to tell the truth. The truth shall set you free. It is not a truth for a truth and a lie for a lie. It is the truth, the whole, truth and nothing but the truth so help you God.'

For the life of me now I can't fully remember what the dispute was about. I think it was that I hadn't turned up for his sports day because my granny was not well, but that could have been another occasion. Or it might have been when Dinko threw my homework copy in the river as a sacrifice to the ducks. Or when I saw the tinkers fighting and was afraid to pass by. I was no angel but all I remember was that this time I was in the right.

I didn't mind the first few slaps. I was used to those. I also had perfected the knack of letting my hand drop just as the leather descended so as to carry the blow. This was acquired from years of observation and then of practice. The art of riding the blows was as artistic as scoring any kind of goals in the slurp of a Saturday afternoon. Some hopped on one leg as if gravity had something to do with it. Others perfected a kind of violin glide close to the jaw which ensured that the blow didn't travel far. Even now I curse every teacher who beat the love of God into me. And yet I thanked them that I gave up education before it rotted the humanity in me. What hurt most in this case was the barb, the accusation, the insult.

One of my friends had met an old terrorist Brother whose motor bike had broken down on the street a few years after he left the school. He kicked it and cursed it and pushed it and then ordered help from his past pupil.

'Brother,' he said, as he stood over him having grown three feet since he left school, 'I wouldn't feed you with snots if you were dying of hunger and I wouldn't ask you to pull me into the last tree house in the universe if the world was drowning in shit. Why not try walking as your limbs have had plenty of exercise?'

'Admit you're a liar, Mac' he had said to me. "Say 'I'm a liar, Brother" and then all will be well.'

But I wouldn't. I knew I was right and that right would always win in the end. We were always taught that justice was the strongest feeling in the world and I used to believe it. Do what's right even if the world should end.

'Say "I'm a liar, Brother," and then I'll stop.'

I couldn't say it. I don't know how long he kept it up but I remember my hands were so numb they hardly existed. I saw the hate and fury in his eyes as he raised the leather again and again and shouted louder each time. If it was a matter of mind versus body I was determined that my mind would not give in first. After all I had right on my side. How come he didn't know that I would die rather than submit? Had they not taught me this?

'Say "I'm a liar, Brother", say it out loud and all will be well.'

My hands swelled up like a boxer's after a fight and would not stay open any more. Some boys put them in under their bums to quell the pain, and others under their armpits, and others spat on them hoping they would not hiss. I always held them up to the air hoping they would heat the world.

It was then he began to hit me anywhere and with anything. When I recovered in the principal's office I had a black eye, a bruised shoulder and there was blood on my ear. My father took me out of school and I never went back. That is why I became a travelling salesman for baby products instead of a banker or a biologist or an engineer. But I had learnt the value of the judicious lie.

'And you didn't go and face him with it?' I asked, 'You didn't have it out with him?'

'You know the way it is,' he said, his dejection spreading from his face all over his body, 'the teacher is always right. Complain and it is even worse for the kid. And besides, this brute wipes the floor with you. He gobbles up parents too.'

'Does he now,' I said, the pain of yesteryear searing through my memory. My hands hurt and I felt as though my eye was beginning to swell. The lump in my throat became hard and and then sore and then tender. 'Well, I think we'll see that times have changed.'

I presented myself at the monastery first thing in the morning before breakfast or school and asked for Brother

Baywolf by his correct name. I was led through a dull corridor with large statues threatening me. Plastered effigies remained sober in the eternally grey passage. A young brother brought me into a spartan sitting room with four straight-backed chairs and a large mahogany table on which stood a vase of artificial flowers. Somebody had sprayed deoderant on them in the hope that they might smell. The carpet was of a kind of greyish green you might see on a bad football pitch on a misty day. A bell rang somewhere in the building and for a second I thought I got the smell of food frying. There were small panes of glass in the window through which I could see a dog licking the footpath. A black car drove slowly down the main street, then gunned its engine and sped quickly into the countryside. I had well rehearsed what I would say and I did not care too much if the suppressed anger of years burst out into whatever form it might. Teachers too had to learn; they had to learn that their pupils always grew up; they had to learn that some scars never healed. I fidgeted with a copy of a religious magazine which dealt with the missions and then threw it from me on to another chair. There was much in it about the love of God but the print was smirched and smudged.

He came in brusquely chewing something in his mouth.

'Well, what is it? You were looking for me?'

It was him all right. It was funny how teachers never changed. They took on a settled appearance in their mid-twenties and stuck with it until retirement. The same banalities for the same thirty or forty years screwed up their brains and allowed them to die before the undertaker got his hands on them. Did they ever stop to ask themselves did they believe it all?

Maybe his glasses were thicker or his eyes had sunken deeper into his head but the rest of him was just the same.

'I'm the father of one of your pupils.'

'Yes.' That one word carried impatience, aggression and an authority that had never been questioned.

'I wanted to inquire about something.'

'Was he impertinent? Does he give trouble at home?'

'No, it wasn't that.'

'Is he not doing his work? We can fix that.'

'Not really.'

His voice softened ever so slightly. Water flowed over rocks and birds sang hundreds of years ago. A heron raised his head from the rushes and a robin trilled high in the tree.

'It wouldn't be anything of a more intimate nature, something you're ashamed of. You can always tell me, you know. I've done a course in parenting.'

It was only then that I noticed on the sleeve of his soutane a big yellow stain. It ran down from his elbow and turned in under his wrist. A bit like the map of Chile but not quite as regular. There may have been some green through it also but I didn't wish to look closely. It was not this morning's egg but must have been encrusted there for weeks. There were gaps in the yellow streak as if he had been picking at it.

'It doesn't really matter,' I said hastily, 'I think it must be a different Brother. I'm sure I have made a mistake.'

'I'm sure you have and thank you for wasting my time,' he said sharply, then turned on his heel and strode out.

I decided not to have any breakfast but to leave the town as quickly as possible. As I walked down the grey steps from the monastery I blew cooly into my hands. A greasy yellow sun dripped over the hills from the east.

Tale in Twenty-Five Words

THE BONE MAN SPENT HIS LIFE examining the dry bones.

One day he saw a real live animal.

He hadn't a clue what it was.

What is to be Done

(from the play Tagann Godot / Godot Turns Up/ Arriva Godot)

THERE WAS THIS MAN ONCE UPON a time and he was very confused.

He searched through the libraries of the world and the scrolls of the scribes but he got no answer. And he studied with the wise professors of learning in the best institutions of knowledge and got no answer. And he starved himself for forty days and nights and even took little pinches of mescalin to open the doors of perception but still he did not get the answer he desired.

So he decided to go on his way and walk from the top of the world to the bottom of the world in order to see could he meet anyone who might answer his question.

And on his way he met an important rich man with moneybags under his eyes and with golden threads through his hair. And he asked of him gently and with proper manners, 'Kind sir,' he said, 'you are a man of the world. You go here, there, and everywhere. You breakfast in London and dine in Montivedeo. You have enough money to break the bank at Monte Carlo or to play footsie with the stock exchange. Would you mind telling me, please, what this is all about, what is the meaning of life?'

And he looked into the eyes of the rich man and he saw the money dancing in them.

And the rich man said to him as he might say to his underlings: 'Sorry boy. Go away. I am too busy. I have to buy another bank. And anyway, it's a stupid question.'

And when he left the place he heard the rich man laugh, and his laugh shook the ground beneath his feet.

And after that he went to The Palace of the King. The King was within perusing a map under eyebrows that looked like moving forests. His fingernails curled like dragons on his abacus as he counted his soldiers. And as he perused with pleasure his forehead took on the contours of an unconquered country and his teeth glistened like burnished shields.

And the man asked him with suitable obsequiousness but in all honesty, 'Your most worthy and inestimable excellency,' he said, 'you are the ruler of many kingdoms. You say to men come and they come, and go to war and they go to war. There is nobody but that does not bow down before your might and majesty and do your bidding. Please, please tell me, what this is all about, what is the meaning of life?'

And he looked into the depths of the eyes of the king and he saw power dancing within.

And the King said to him with suitable royal impatience: 'Begone from here, you fool, before I chop off your head. Don't you see that I am too busy erecting monuments and defeating knavish enemies? And anyway, it is a stupid question.'

And when he left that place he could hear the King and his courtiers laughing and their laughs echoed like trampling hooves on the flagstones of the road.

And after that he went to the Temple. The Chief Priest was within praying on his bended knees. And the man spoke to him and said: 'Your most benign grace and utmost holiness,' he said, 'you have read all the books of theology and the scrolls of scripture. You know the lives of the saints and the prognostications of the prophets. You offer sacrifices and make obeisances daily. You fast and abstain. You keep the ten commandments and possess the seven gifts of the holy ghost and practise the cardinal virtues. Can you please, please, tell me what this is all about, what is the meaning of life?'

And he peered down into the eyes of the Chief Priest and he saw sanctity and holiness dancing madly in them.

And the Chief Priest said to him with authority: 'Depart from me before I set the faithful upon you. Dost thou not see that I am too busy adoring God? I have to make reparations for the sins of the world. And anyway, it is a stupid question.'

And when he left that place with a troubled heart he heard the Chief Priest laughing, and his laugh drew echoes down from the speedwell blue of the sky.

And outside of the Temple he saw a small boy begging.

'Help me,' said the boy, 'I have had nothing to drink for three days and I am dying of thirst.'

And when the man saw the wretchedness of the boy he cried bitterly. And he filled a cup with his tears and he gave it to the boy and the boy drank it and was grateful.

And now I ask you, which of these people did most good, the men who laughed, or the man who cried?

What's Left of Us

'WHAT AM I DOING AT ALL, at all, on this earth of ours,' the big lumbering dinosaur began to ask himself, 'if my lot and kind are bound for imminent extinction?'

This little thought caused him great anguish and woe and mental pain so that he piddled down his rear left leg, such was the wind at the time.

Some millions of years after that the shine of his piss could be observed on the ear-rings of the princess as she drove into the tunnel.

Translations

THE PEOPLE WERE ROUNDED UP AFTER the battle. They were hauled up out of their hovels and holes by the point of a bayonet. Some of them muttering prayers. Others curses. Some trying to keep their children quiet. Others letting them cry as if it was the last thing they would do. A woman who smothered her child trying now to revive her. A man who believed in the prophecies desperately trying to recall what they were.

They were ushered into the barn. The air was thick with crying. A priest comforting them with the thought of eternal life. Another kept his hand in his mouth.

The sergeant stood before them with the authority of victory. 'Now my worthies,' he bellowed, with what might now be called irony dripping from his lips, 'what hath ye to say in yere defence?' Few understood his words, but they read his voice. They did not reply.

Later when one old man tried to explain about his daughter and why she shouldn't be taken away only stuttering jabber came from his lips. When the priest spoke of mercy in his broken English they cut out his tongue.

When the soldiers saw how neat and easy it was to cut out a tongue they went to work. The tongues fell to the floor to be collected and fed to the horses. Nothing was now heard in the barn except the wailing of bloody mouths and the gnashing of bloody gums.

'Speak now,' said the sergeant to them, 'if ye hath anything to say.'

'What didst I tell thee,' he said to his servant, 'this be a culture that is absolutely dumb. Who wilt know the difference when we silence it forever?'

Buried Treasure

AFTERWARDS, IT LOOKED LIKE A SHABBY derelict cottage with dirty flaking lime coming off the wall in scabs. Then it was the very picture of a beautiful country house with whitewashed walls and a thatched roof like you would see on a tourist's postcard. Afterwards, when I went back the roof was covered in rusting corrugated iron and bales of straw filled the parlour. Then a beautiful flower garden spilled out from the back of the house and the smell of roses hung about the eaves.

It is a mystery how the sharp eggshells of memory stick when the general picture remains clouded. I do not know why I remember clearly an old mouldy saddle in the barn as if somebody there had once ridden a horse when the rest of that place is now dark. Or the chamber pot which Bridie used for bringing in water from the well. Or the wooden cradle which she used for keeping turf. Or the bellows with the leather thongs like a rats tail beside the fire. Or the string, which was mended in three places, which Johnny used to keep his trousers up when working. I also remember certain smells and tastes which have never been repeated and are never likely to be.

I was out hunting for rabbits when I met Johnny on the

way back. I wasn't really hunting for rabbits but just staying out of the adults' way and pretending to explore the hillside and the valley that I knew quite well from previous visits. But there was always the chance that I might catch one and that would have been a greater act of heroism than the slaughtering of hordes of Vikings or marauding pirates that I was normally engaged in. And, anyway, rabbits were so new and so strange to me that chasing them was as exciting an experience as conquering any invaders my imagination could call up.

'Stay away from the bull in the shcrohach field,' Johnny said to me.

'I wasn't near there at all,' I said. 'I've been well warned.'

'And some of them cows are none too peaceful either,' he said, resting on his spade. 'A mad cow can be worse than a bull, just as a mad woman can be worse than any man.'

I shuddered a little at that because I had been out among the cows earlier and one of them had followed me all the way to the ditch. Also, I heard my aunt say that Bridie was mad and they always spoke about her in mysterious tones. She certainly cackled loudly and exposed her pink mouth like a horse when she laughed. And she laughed a lot more than most adults I have known.

Johnny didn't laugh. But when he smiled two spiders appeared on the corners of his mouth and wriggled slightly. He was smiling now.

'Do you see that?' he asked me.

I could see nothing only the wet black soil he had turned over with his spade.

'No,' I said, not knowing what I was supposed to see. He had shown me my first robin's nest the year before and had taught me how to recognise a badger's lair.

'You townies see nothing,' he said. 'Look again and you will see a worm.'

I did now but it was the colour of the black earth and barely bothering to move as if it was entirely at home.

'That's a sign of good soil,' he said proudly, 'This is the only patch of good soil I have in the whole place.'

'How far down are you going to dig?' I asked him, and it was only then I realised why I had asked him the question.

'I only turn over the sod.' He took out his pipe and shook the dottle on the air. 'That's all it needs. Show the good soil the sun and it will do everything you ask.'

The fragile bleat of a sheep could be heard on a distant hill and I got the impression that blood had entered the evening colours.

'It must be nearly time for us to go back now,' he said, 'Your father will be coming to collect you soon.'

The cottage was far from any proper roads and my father had to drive down a boreen that had a stream running on it to get anywhere near us. Even then we had to walk over several fields to get to the car. I once saw a nanny-goat who had just given birth to her kid in the corner of one of those fields. It was there also that I first handled the soft slobber of frog spawn in the slush of the river.

'I was just wondering,' I said, not knowing if I should say it or not, 'I was just wondering if you dug deep enough would you get any treasure?'

This time he laughed. He could open and close his eyes

like a cat but there was always a glint in them.'The only treasure you will get around here is the earth itself. And nobody seems to want that anymore.'

I still had my doubts. My aunt always believed that Bridie and Johnny were loaded with money. She said they kept it in their mattress or in tin cans in a secret hole in the wall. You knew she felt it was a tragedy that all that money was not being used. I remember finding a tin can in the outhouse and prising it open with excitement but it only contained a crust of hard stale mustard.

'Bridie will get you something to eat,' he said, 'you must be starving after all that running.'

I was starving but I didn't want to tell him I wasn't hugely looking forward to what Bridie might give me. She was the first person to give me turnip soup and I am glad to say the last. Her brown cake was alright if you managed to get your teeth into the middle but the wedge of home made butter which smothered it might contain anything from a hair to a midge.

Although evening was approaching honeysuckle still speckled the hedges and white violets as round and plump as a cushion sat in the corners of the fields. A drift of ducks passed us by filling the ditches with their gabble. We walked on rock and then on spongy wet ground green with sopping mosses.

When we reached the cottage the lamp was just being lit and faces flickered inside like shadows on a windowpane. I felt drugged with fresh air and was happy to sit on the settle with my legs dangling.

'He'll sing a song,' said my aunt, pushy as usual. The others said nothing as they were more used to me. I knew this was coming so I sang something I had learnt at school just to get it over with.

'That's a great boy,' said Bridie, her cheeks like a polished apple gleaming at me. 'I think you deserve something special.'

She brought me a stone mug of buttermilk and her big curdled face was alight with life. I couldn't refuse but the first sip nearly made me retch. When she went to get Johnny his braces I slipped out the door and poured the rest of it into the trough.

My aunt was singing. I think it was 'How Can You Buy Killarney' because even then I knew it was corny. Or it may have been 'If We Only Had Old Ireland Over Here'. Even though she was home from the States on a holiday I don't suppose she was too troubled if the sentimentality was Australian.

I stayed at the door. A moon with a ripe edge on it rose behind the thorn tree whose branches spread out like wrinkles on the night. A swill of light spilt across the brow of the hill. It must have been a lone car cutting the evening. As I looked out over that hill my bones always felt small and insignificant. A moth birring softly on the cottage window was the only opposition to my aunt's singing. I could see her skin like underdone pastry from where I stood, and her mouth moved in tune with a record she had heard so often. Her lipstick matched her red shoes and her glasses were shaped like butterfly's wings. I picked flakes from the whitewashed wall. Some of them came away like the crumbly biscuits Bridie kept for special occasions.

When the clap finished somebody asked Bridie to sing.

'There's no need, really,' I heard my aunt say in her American drawl, 'We'll have to be going soon. The car should be at the top of the boreen by now.'

But she sang anyway. I had never heard her sing before and when her voice opened I felt a strange tingling in my throat. It was a kind of singing completely foreign to me. The tune took off for a phrase and then suddenly stopped. She seemed to pause in all the wrong places. She hummed on consonants as if kissing them. The song wandered and hesitated and rested and cantered. Then it soared with the wind and plunged like a hawk before her voice hugged a word as if she would never let it go. Then it mounted and swooped again in a different sinuous arabesque. From time to time a vowel would quiver as if in anger and then it made sweet moan as it vanished into another sound. It wreathed and weaved through a skein of cadences and wound tendrils around tones that anyone else would have sung straight. Every few notes she lingered vibrating softly on a sound like a cat purring. Nor do I remember what the words were about. All I can recall is that there were some I could not understand at all even though their sounds were familiar. She finished with a clump of notes like a honey bee turning and twisting into the sky and her voice trembled like the golden flames of a lonely candle in a dark church.

I think there may have been a polite clap but it was very brief.

I heard my aunt say, 'Wouldn't you think we have enough of all those come-all-yes by now? We want something modern.' The air seethed between them.

Somebody else said, 'That stuff is all dead and buried by

now. The boy doesn't want to hear any moaning and groaning.'

I didn't mind, but when I looked in I saw everybody gabbling away while Bridie was stooped down cleaning some ash from the grate. I felt badly when I gave her back the empty mug.

Some years later when she died a few weeks after Johnny we went back to the house. It seemed smaller and diminished but everything does as you get older. The grass couch across from the front door appeared more bare and even the walls of the cottage were turning sere under the eaves. What shocked us most was that the place had been ransacked. In the kitchen the settle had been overturned and the sideboard with the delph cast on its side. Some bricks had been removed from behind the fireplace and the mattress in the bedroom had been filleted and ripped asunder. An empty biscuit tin lay naked at the foot of the stairs to the loft. My aunt looked angry and tightlipped although she couldn't admit she was bitter that somebody got there before her.

'I wonder did they get anything?' she asked.

'They got nothing,' my father said with authority. 'There was nothing to get. They never had a tosser between them. How could they? Two old people on a small holding with barely enough to keep body and soul together. People love to think that everyone else has bags of money.'

'The old crone,' my aunt said with some spite, 'Knowing her, whatever treasure she had she took it with her.'

She didn't know that she never spoke a truer word, but I don't suppose anything I might say could ever have made her realise it. When she turned on the radio in the car on the way home I could only remember the flight of the honey bee rising and twisting into the air over the flowers behind the house which had the scent of roses hanging all about it.

The Troublesome Young Woman

THERE WAS ONCE A TROUBLESOME young woman whom her parents called a little bitch. Others called her other things but as her parents loved her dearly it was enough to call her a little bitch. And because they loved her dearly they did not throw her on the street even when she constantly stole their credit cards, crashed her mother's car, ripped her father's clothes, called them stupid fucking wrinklies and acted the general, well, bitch. But because they loved her dearly they would do anything to help her and even went so far as to bring her to a psychiatrist.

'It's penis envy,' he said, 'no doubt about it. I've seen it many times before. Young women her age all suffer from it even if they don't admit it. And just because they don't admit it doesn't mean they don't suffer from it. Nothing here that a good man and a good bit of bonking will not cure.'

Because they loved her and because they were paying good money to the psychiatrist they let her out about the town with as much money to visit the best night clubs and stay in the best hotels as she wanted. Not that she needed any urging nor advice about where to go. But it was nice to be able to do it with her parents' (and the psychiatrist's) permission.

She had a ball of a time with big hunky macho muscular types and long wiry athletic fitfreaks and flashy moneyed longpracticed swingers for as long as she could and wanted. After that she came home and put the cat in the microwave oven, cut the heads off all the roses, gouged the tyres of her daddy's car, pissed in her mother's swimming pool and generally acted the, well, bitch.

Because they loved her and were paying good money they brought her back to the psychiatrist.

'It wasn't penis envy,' said her father without going into much detail, 'of that we can be absolutely sure.'

'Well if it wasn't penis envy,' said the psychiatrist, 'it must be something else. Wait till I see.'

And he took a big leatherbound book down from the shelf.

These Two Guys

THERE WERE THESE TWO GUYS WHO lived out in the country not far from the city to where they could commute. They were good friends. They often went hill-walking together, and hunting, and fishing. But more than anything else they loved to swim in the river which ran beside the meadow near where they lived not far from the city to which they could commute.

Let us call them Luke and David. We may call Luke Luke because he always looked before he leaped whereas David was David because he dived in without looking.

They did used to have great fun swimming from bank to bank, watching the lambs frolicking and gambolling in the fields, and the calves lowing in the slanting meadows, and the women sowing and reaping as they solitarily sang of far-off happy things and battles long ago, and the thrushes chirping on the boughs, and all that kind of stuff.

They were happy and content like this for a long time, it did seem like hundreds of years, until Luke copped that something was bugging Dave.

'Dave,' he asked, directly, 'What's up?'

'Nothing's up,' said Dave, with some sense of structure, 'everything is down. It's like this. We are only swimming on the surface. We are hardly scraping the lid, so to speak. Think of all that is hidden from us down in the depths. I was always told to go down deep. To get to another level. To get to the bottom of things. And anyway, I'm pissed off with the view around these parts. Same old trees of green and skies of blue and clouds of white. Same old bright blessed day and dark dingy night. It might be a wonderful world but I have enough of it. I want something else.'

And just like that he stuck his arse in the air and dived down, down, down to where the fish flashed through the muddy murk and down, down, down to where the eels lurked in the slobby slurk and down, down, down in the nether darkness above the globby gluck which everybody thinks holds the junk and bunk and old boots in the holes at the bottom of the world.

We do not know what he saw or what he discovered or what he found because it seems that he never came back to tell the tale.

Luke, however, stayed on the surface all this time getting a suntan, and splashing the water on his body, and watching the lambs gambolling in the fields, and listening to the calves lowing in the slanting meadows, and the women solitarily sowing and reaping and singing of far-off happy things and battles long-ago, and the thrushes chirping on the boughs, and all that kind of stuff.

It is, of course, always possible that Dave got to the bottom of things.

It is also possible, of course, that he is still chasing a bottom that is always moving away.

The Brotherhood of Wisdom

ONCE UPON A TIME IN A kingdom in which there were no newspapers lived a man who wished to acquire wisdom. He spent all of his time from the breaking of the day to the making of the night travelling around to the bearded wise ones who wore sandals and spoke in cryptic monosyllables. He sat at their feet and drank deeply of the words which fell from their mouths.

He read all the great manuscripts and great books of wisdom in the great libraries of that great kingdom. He was awarded high honours in the public examinations for degrees and diplomas in wisdom and wore the red robes of those who had successfully completed their studies in wisdom accordingly.

He was rightly and justly and meetly proud of his achievements in wisdom studies. He attended wisdom conferences in many parts of the world and wrote wisdom monographs with neatly arranged footnotes which were always consistent in style and lay-out.

Despite this, however, and despite the kinds of kudos (at least) which he got at dinner parties and fancy receptions when people asked him what his field of expertise was and he could answer with an owlish shrug, 'Well, wisdom, actually,' despite all this he desperately wished to be accepted into The Brotherhood of Wisdom so that he could spend the rest of his mortal days listening to those whose every thought sprang from the wellsprings of inspiration and whose every moment was founded in the wellfount of truth.

He spent forty days crossing the desert on a horse with no name and it was good to be out of the rain even if he only ate withered figs and drank camel piss. In the end he reached the monastery of the Brotherhood of Wisdom somewhere between the sea and the mountains.

He was allowed in and asked all the hard questions.

And he had all the answers. He sang for them the psalms of the prophets and sighed the sayings of the seers amd mumbled the mantras of the mysterious. He gave out bits of the silver apples of thc moon and put before them chunks of the golden apples of the sun. He spoke of the ox of the seven combats and refuted the beasts out of anima mundi. All this and much more he knew in his head because he had cogitated thereupon and had gained first-class honours in his examinations in the study of wisdom.

'Very well, then,' said the carbuncular Abbot, 'it doth appear that you do know it all. But there is yet one more test that you have to do, one more trial for you to essay before you are allowed into the Brotherhood of Wisdom. Come hither.'

And the man went to him very quickly indeed and with great eagerness and the Abbot looked down into his throat.

'Hmm,' he said whilst he thought and looked and

produced the lighted reed which was always on hand on occasions like this. He plunged the reed down the man's throat and when he withdrew it was utterly quenched.

'You've failed,' the Abbot said roughly, 'depart and remove and vanish from this place and out of my sight.'

'But, but, but,' the man said a few more times, 'I have all the knowledge, I have read all the books, I have answered all the questions, I have supped at the feet of the wise, I have followed all the instructions, I have completed all my courses and gained all my degress, diplomas and certificates with the highest of distinctions and merits and honours. Why then are you banishing me?'

'Because you have no wick,' said the Abbot.

And then the man picked up his bags and went away and his heart was heavy and sore. And as he crossed the bridge it gave way and he fell down into the rushing stream.

And he drowned therein because he could not swim with the weight which he carried in his soul.

An Explosion of Skylarks

I KNEW MY GRANNY WAS NOT well by the hushed tones of my aunts and the serious faces of the neighbours. People were coming and going to the room for days and nobody seemed any happier.

I didn't mind too much as it gave me a chance to wander through the fields on my own, something I would never be allowed to do in the city. It was good to be forgotten about sometimes, although I would never admit it out loud. The only other child brought here was Aunt Peggy's Danny and he was always stuck in a book. I knew he was boring the first time I saw him by the kind of glasses he wore.

Granny also wore glasses but she wasn't wearing them when my mother brought me in to see her.

'Come and see granny,' she said, as I was sitting on the bank outside the cottage looking for ladybirds and watching for the numbers of the cars which never seemed to pass by. For some reason it seemed a long journey through the flagstoned kitchen up to the bedroom beyond the dresser and around the table where a plate of potatoes in their jackets waited to be undressed. Two old men sat silently on the settle clutching their walking sticks between their knees.

Granny lay in her large bed with the bolster behind her head and with a quilt the colour of the countryside up to her neck. I had never really seen her eyes before as her glasses were as thick as bottle-bottoms and now they were closed like a bad stitch in a piece of linen.

'It's Sarah, gran,' my mother said, drawing me up closer to the bed and laying my hand on her cold arm.

The stitches opened and two eyes the colour of cheese flickered for me.

'Good girl, Sarah,' her voice said weakly, 'good girl.'

I didn't know what to say but for some silly reason I kept thinking of the big bad wolf and a basket of food. She may have tried to smile but her teeth looked rusted and she closed her eyes again with the effort.

'Tell gran what you have been doing,' my mother said, giving me a little nudge.

Granny wasn't saying anything but seemed to be waiting for me to speak and I desperately wanted somebody to say something.

'I've just been wandering about I suppose,' I said. 'I was down in the brake the other day picking blackberries. I saw the calves in Leonard's field. They were lovely. Maggie Carroll showed me all the hens and I helped her feed the turkeys. I messed around with the old wheel in the cart shed yesterday. I helped Johnny Carey check up on his sheep over by the bridge and I was talking to an old man with a red beard and a dog up near Griffin's on the way home.'

I didn't know what else I should say but granny's eyes were suddenly staring at me, if I could call the deep grey look she gave me a stare. Then she turned her head slowly towards the wall and the rims of her eyes were a red I had never seen before.

'That'll do now, Sarah,' my mother said, lifting me up and ushering me out. 'Gran's too tired for all that talk. Go away and play, but don't go too far.'

I was going to say that I didn't want to talk at all but somehow I felt that the time wasn't right. I wandered out to the back field but Danny spoiled the view.

'What's the book, Danny?' I said, just to interrupt him.

'Nothing you would be interested in,' he said, adjusting his glasses so that he could see me and the print at the same time.

'Try me.'

'It's psychology,' he said, 'The Theory of Mind.'

'Yuk!' I replied. 'How boring!'

I skipped off down between the row of beech trees that divided the meadow from the rough bracken that fell away towards the stream. I didn't really care where I was going, but I knew I needed a lot of air. The sky above me was wide and flat and a watery sun dripped above the trees. It seemed to me as if some of the tall bushes were exotic animals with wild hair blowing in the breeze, the trees strange creatures with dry horns stabbing the sky. I filled my lungs with the good air and plunged headlong down the glen before the trees and the sky could press upon me.

I had come across the well before but it had never seemed so clear. I cupped my hands and sipped the water which was as clean and sharp as a knife. It was refreshing to lie back on a cool patch of grass and listen to the water ribbing the rocks in the stream and dream of nothing in particular. Overhead an acorn shaped like a tear hung from a branch but it did not fall which made me very happy. I was not really a loner, but there were times when walking through the lush clover, or just swinging your arms this way and that, or closing your eyes in the heather was the most perfect thing to do.

When I felt a cloud across the sun I got up and continued down the glen. I had not been this way before and so I became excited by the silence which was in full leaf around me. For a while I could hear no birds, the stream had gone underground and the light breeze had been choked in the thick gorse. I knew that life moved in the soft mould and in the undergrowth but it was all quiet like fingers in velvet.

'It's you again!'

The voice boomed at me as if it was coming from a deep cave and I would have turned and fled if it wasn't for the smile on his face. Although he was old his teeth were as white as salt and his red beard could have been on fire. Huge tufts of growth stood out from where his eyebrows should be and his eyes flashed like trout in a sunlit stream.

'I'm sorry,' I said, 'I didn't know anybody lived down here. I didn't mean to intrude.'

'Don't apologise,' he said, his voice rumbling as if it carried rocks in its wake, 'Don't go around making excuses for yourself or you'll never see the sky.'

I wasn't quite sure what he meant but he said it kindly. He was sitting outside his cottage scratching his dog who hadn't woken up when I approached and even appeared more hairy than the old man himself. The cottage was of flaked whitewash with a corrugated iron roof that had a few sods thrown on top as if some big bird had deposited them there.

'Like a cup of milk?' he asked, 'you've been running.'

'Yes, please,' I said, as I couldn't just turn on my heel and return back up the glen.

He vanished into the cottage and brought out two mugs of milk. He drank from his quickly and gave the rest to the dog. I put mine to my lips and spluttered when the first taste entered my mouth.

'Never drank goat's milk before?' he asked.

'It's awful,' I said, 'why haven't you got a cow?'

'Because I have a goat,' he said.

'Then you're not a real farmer,' I said. 'Real farmers have cows.'

I heard him chuckle at that, and he scratched the dog a little more vigorously as if to get him to share in the joke.

'You think everyone in the country is a farmer, then?' he said, 'where did you read that? In a book?'

The word book seemed to hop off the ground but the smile was still on his face. A hen came out of the door of the cottage and scratched at the earthen threshold. The soft warm smell of turf passed me by on the breeze on its way out towards the crown of the moor.

'Might have,' I said, 'what's wrong with that?'

'Everything,' he said, stretching out his hand and clutching the hen by the neck. He stroked it gently as if it was a pet cat and cooed quietly into its feathers. 'If you read it in a book it's wrong.'

'That's crazy,' I said, 'our teacher told us we should read all the time. That way we'll learn about the world.'

'Why don't you just open your eyes,' he said. 'Why don't

you just think? You don't need books to think. Everything is all around you.' He swept his loose hand up to the sky, down past the forehead of the hill, across the woods and it landed again on the black loam under his boot. 'I suppose you're good at school?'

'I'm o.k. I don't mind it.'

'Are you going to be a schoolteacher too? Like your grandfather.'

'I don't know. I've never thought about it.'

'Don't.'

He said it like a command, like an old prophet in a green world. Even though his voice was controlled his eyes looked as if they were wrestling with a tomcat.

'Ever seen the inside of a teachers head?' he asked, and I knew it was a question I wouldn't have a chance to answer. 'All laid out in parts like a classroom. Dry as a blackboard. Lined like a rollbook. Nothing gets in there except through the pages of a book, and a book is the prison of knowledge. Traps the soul and locks it up.'

His huge lardlike shoulders heaved while he took in his breath and he hitched up the coarse sacking around his waist. A second hen came out of the house and scratched at the bare dock roots in the sour earth outside the door. I could just see an iron pot hanging from a soot-covered chain above the fireplace but the rest was darkness.

Just then he raised the hen to his mouth and dug his teeth into its neck. Head and body broke apart like he was tearing paper, and blood bubbled at the corner of his mouth.

'Ever eat a real chicken?' he snorted, but I turned and fled. I crashed through a wall of brambles and stumbled up the hill without once looking back. I knew he was too old to follow but a red beard flecked with blood kept looming up at me from the trees. I charged through the unmown fields and under the green hollies on the edge of the stream. I didn't feel safe until I saw the house beyond me on the slope of the ridge.

A dry light hovered over the roof and I could see my mother at the door talking to a priest. I ran headlong across the field to the house shouting as I went. Suddenly the grass around me seemed to explode as hundreds of birds rose up into the sky. I didn't stop to pick up Danny's book in my flight.

ABOUT ALAN TITLEY

Alan Titley is a novelist, story writer, playwright and scholar. He has also written and presented documentary films on literary and historical subjects, and has been writing a weekly column for the *Irish Times* on current and cultural matters since 2003.

He was born and raised in Cork city, initially studied to be a primary school teacher, and taught in Nigeria during the Biafran War. While there he travelled extensively in West Africa in both the jungle and the desert. He returned and taught deaf children in Dublin while studying for an evening degree in University College Dublin. Was appointed as a lecturer in Irish in St Patrick's College, Drumcondra in 1974, and Head of Department in 1981. He became Professor of Modern Irish in University College Cork in 2006, a position from which he has recently retired. He was elected a Member of the Royal Irish Academy in 2012.

He writes mainly in Irish, but Lagan Press has published a selection of his stories and fables in English in *Parabolas*, and a large selection of his critical and cultural essays in *Nailing Theses* (2011). His six novels include two for children, one of which *Amach* ('Out') won the Éilís Dillon Award in 2004, and his latest *Smuf* (2012) concerns a dog with a muffled bark who has been abandoned by its owners. Two of his novels have an African background: *Méirscrí na Treibhe* ('Tribal Scars') deals with troubling politics in a newly independent African state; and *Gluaiseacht* ('Moving') tells the story of young African children leaving their home for a new life somewhere in Europe. *An Fear Dána* (1993) is a novel re-imagining the life of the 13th century Irish and Scottish poet Muiríoch Albanach Ó Dálaigh, which includes murder, sex, poetry and mystery.

One of his collections of stories *Leabhar Nóra Ní Anluain* ('Nora Hanlon's Book') contains more than a hundred stories, while *Eiriceachtaí agus Scéalta Eile* ('Heresies and Other Stories') won the Butler Prize from the Irish-American Cultural Institute.

His plays include *Tagann Godot* ('Godot Turns Up'), which is a sequel to Samuel Beckett's famous drama, and was produced in the Abbey Peacock in Dublin and has been translated into Russian, Italian and French. *An Ghráin agus an Ghruaim* ('The Hate and the Horrors') won the BBC Stewart Parker Award and is included in *Na Drámaí Garbha* ('The Rough Plays' 2011) a collection of plays on the similar theme of the awfulness of rural life, each one of which has been produced professionally.

Scéal na Gaeilge ('The Story of Irish'), a two-part film, was shown in 2012 on TG4, and tells the course of the Irish language from before to dawn of our history until the present day. It was written and presented by Alan, who also wrote prize-winning documentaries on Liam O'Flaherty, Máirtín Ó Direáin and Máirtín Ó Cadhain. These reflect his scholarly interests in all aspects of modern Irish literature from the thirteenth century on, with a particular emphasis on contemporary writing. *An tÚrscéal Gaeilge* is a comprehensive study of the Irish novel, while Lagan has also published a collection of his critical and cultural essays in *Chun Doirne* ('Fisticuffs'). He has also a lively interest in Scottish literature and as a Corkman is very proud to say that he is being published in the second city of Ireland.

BV - #0043 - 290121 - C0 - 198/129/13 - PB - 9781904652236 - Matt Lamination